KT-436-367

The Three-Cornered Hat

The Three-Cornered Hat

Pedro Antonio de Alarcón

Translated by Peter Bush

ET REMOTISSIMA PROPE

Hesperus Classics

CHARTERHOUSE
LIBRARY

Hesperus Classics
Published by Hesperus Press Limited
4 Rickett Street, London sw6 1ru
www.hesperuspress.com

The Three-Cornered Hat first published in Spanish as *El Sombrero de tres picos* in 1874
This translation first published by Hesperus Press Limited, 2004

Introduction and English language translation © Peter Bush, 2004

Designed and typeset by Fraser Muggeridge
Printed in Italy by Graphic Studio Srl

isbn: 1-84391-080-2

All rights reserved. This book is sold subject to the condition that it shall not be
resold, lent, hired out or otherwise circulated without the express prior consent of the
publisher.

CONTENTS

Picasso, Diaghilev and Manuel de Falla were all drawn to the wit and farcical comedy of Pedro Antonio de Alarcón's *The Three-Cornered Hat*, and helped make it the only work by the Andalusian author to be read widely today. In 1874, when the novel was first published, Spain was still suffering a third Carlist war, though the country had left behind the years of revolutionary republican struggle prompted by the revolution of September 1868, when Marx and Bakunin came to the fore for the first time in Spain (at least till 1936). By now, Alarcón had espoused the monarchist cause of the Spanish Bourbons, but he could still recreate the lecherous, purple-cloaked, cockaded chief magistrate in a final anti-authoritarian flourish which recalled his radical Romantic youth.

Born in 1833 into a modest, once noble family of ten, in the southern town of Guadix – famed for its huge cathedral and community of cave-dwellers – he had not always been a man of order. His paternal grandfather lost all his property and was imprisoned during the Napoleonic invasion; the only family relics of more prosperous times were his grandfather's purple cloak and three-cornered hat from his days as chief magistrate. The young Pedro was not drawn to such symbols of authority hanging up at home. Though his parents sent him to a seminary to encourage a clerical career, he spent his time in the cloisters reading and writing, and by 1853, he had departed to work on the literary supplement of a liberal Cadiz newspaper, *The Western Echo*. Soon he was off to Madrid, with two thousand lines of verse, which he'd written as a continuation of a poem by the Romantic poet José de Espronceda.

A year later he was back in the south – in Granada, where *The Western Echo* had also relocated – and as a young romantic he supported the liberal revolution of 1854. In the thick of the fighting, Alarcón led an attack on an arms depot and distributed guns to the insurgent populace. He also helped found an anti-clerical, anti-army newspaper called *Redemption*. During his militant years in Granada (1853–63) as a member of the revolutionary group of intellectuals known as the 'Granadan Rope', he befriended a liberal intellectual named Giner de los Ríos, a pioneer of European thought in Spain and the ideological grandfather of the university residency which brought Lorca, Buñuel and Dalí together in the 1920s.

Madrid literary life soon beckoned again, and Alarcón was invited to edit the anti-clerical, republican paper *The Whip*, which he later dubbed 'a rabidly demagogic daily'. He rapidly embarked on a conversion to more moderate opinions – a conversion he always denied. It seems a turning point was a rash duel with a Venezuelan absolutist who, more expert than he with the pistol, took pity and fired over his head and not at his heart. Alarcón enlisted in General O'Donnell's African campaign in a frenzy of patriotic fervour which inspired his *Diary of a Witness to the War in Africa*, which sold over fifty thousand copies. The consequent royalties enabled him to tour Italy and France and earn a reputation as a travel writer. As a politician he joined the Liberal Union, was elected member of parliament for Guadix, and entered the literary salons of Madrid society. However, his move to the right was tempered by the rise of 'iron surgeon' General Narváez and in 1866, even he had to go into exile.

During the period opened up by the Glorious Revolution of September 1868, by which time he had returned to Madrid, Alarcón championed a renovation of the monarchy through Alfonso's succession to the throne of the discredited Isabel II. The first ten years of the ensuing Restoration were a period of intense literary activity for Alarcón. The success of his rambling, right-wing novels was short-lived and he abandoned Madrid in something of a huff even though he had been admitted to the Royal Academy.

He found literary success in 1874 with *The Three-Cornered Hat*, which went through eight editions in ten years and was translated into ten languages. It was as if Alarcón had tapped into the vein, opened by French and German Romantics, of a European love for the exoticism of Spain. His tale of intrigue and the seduction of a miller's wife by a magistrate draws on a Spanish tradition of oral and written ballads dating back to the Middle Ages, though the book is not without a hint of Beaumarchais's Bartholo or Molière's Tartuffe. His genius was to implant the popular story into a historical setting at the beginning of the nineteenth century, when the Inquisition was in full swing and law enforcers were often less than legal in their actions on behalf of their own authority. Alarcón's ironic look at Hispanic backwardness draws on his own family's painful experience of the Napoleonic invasion.

While the third Carlist war raged until 1876, nostalgia for Inquisitional times was still rife in some quarters. Though the location of the story is vaguely Andalusian – a mill near Guadix or near Granada – the provenance of the protagonists is reiterated. The magistrate is from Madrid, symbol of a centralist government, seat of power of the monarchy and Inquisition. Frasquita, the miller's wife, has abandoned Estella, a Navarran citadel of Carlist agitation, and one reason for her eagerness to get her nephew appointed in the south is to spare him that variety of retro-Catholicism. The miller, old Lucas, is from Archena, a town in Murcia, an impoverished region much derided by Castile. Though the bucolic paternalism of the clerics who promenade to picnic at the mill and the saintly countenance of the magistrate's wife lend the story Victorian respectability, the irony is sharp at the expense both of Church and State.

Included here are the author's preface and a translation of one of the racier versions of the fable, which Alarcón seems to argue against. His preface is as interesting for what it does not say. While assuring his readers that his version will not make them blush, he fails to mention that his miller's fable is satirically incisive. Unlike the traditional ballads, which are generally anti-authority and never fixed historically, his frame is specific and linked to institutions that still invoked loyal allegiances and bellicose passions. Similarly, though the sexual come-ons are mild rather than provocative, Frasquita does flaunt her body to get her way and the saintly Doña Mercedes is prepared to stage the charade of sharing her bed with the miller in order to humiliate her husband.

His tale was and is an invitation to readers to look up a ballad tradition which in Spain was prolonged well into the twentieth century. The nineteenth-century version celebrates a wife-swapping episode that is distinctly moulded against concern for masculine honour and revenge. The sexual levity and forwardness of its female protagonists are part of a Hispanic bawdy literary tradition frequently concealed by the convention that prefers Spain to be different (and Catholic). Even today, flamenco singers tell of the wife of the miller from Arcos who was blonde and hot to trot…

Though Alarcón attenuates the sexual, his story is a farcical comedy of disguises and Punch-and-Judy knockabouts which tilts at the powers-that-be who get into frolics and scrapes of Curry and Major proportions.

– Peter Bush, 2004

The Three-Cornered Hat

Few Spaniards, even among the least learned and well read, are unfamiliar with the coarse little tale which provides the subject for the present trifle.

A rough-and-ready goatherd, who never left the remote farmstead where he was born, was the first person we heard recount it. He was one of those unlettered rustics, naturally gifted at joking and japing, who play such an important role as the picaresque rogues of Spanish literature. Whenever there was a party on the farm, on the occasion of a christening or wedding, or a solemn visitation by the owners, it was his duty to organise games and entertainments, to play the clown and recite ballads and stories, and it was for one such celebration (almost a lifetime... that is, more than thirty-five years ago) that he had the bright idea of bedazzling and garnishing our (relative) innocence one night with the versified tale of *The Magistrate and the Miller's Wife*, or *The Miller and the Magistrate's Wife*, which today we offer to our readers under the more transcendental, philosophical title (in keeping with the gravity of our times) of *The Three-Cornered Hat*.

We recall, moreover, that when the shepherd gave us such a good time, the nubile girls present blushed profusely, and hence their mothers concluded the tale was rather beyond the pale and tried to consign the shepherd to the shadows, yet the hapless Repela (for such was his name) didn't bite his lip but replied by saying there was no reason to be so shocked, for his story contained nothing that nuns and four-year-old girls didn't already know...

'And if not, you tell me,' the goatherd asked, 'what do we learn from the tale of *The Magistrate and the Miller's Wife*? That married people sleep together, and that no husband is amused if another man sleeps with his wife! This is hardly news!…'

'Well, he's right!' replied the mothers, hearing their daughters' loud laughter.

'The proof old Repela is right,' observed the bridegroom's father, 'is that the young and old alike already know that, once the dancing finishes tonight, Juanete and Manolilla will christen this beautiful double bed which Aunt Gabriela has just shown our daughters so they could admire the large, prettily embroidered pillows…'

'And that's not the end of it!' said the bride's grandfather. 'Even the book of Holy Doctrine and sermons during Mass tell children of such natural things, like the protracted barrenness suffered by Our Lady St Anne, chaste Joseph's virtue, Judith's strategem,[1] and many other miracles I forget for the moment. Consequently, ladies and gents…'

'Come on, come on, old Repela!' the girls valiantly exclaimed. 'Tell us your tale again. It's so funny!'

'Not to say very decent!' continued Grandfather. 'For nobody's told to do anything evil; or taught how to be so; nor is anyone left punished who is so…'

'That's right! Give it to us again!' all the matriarchs finally clamoured in concert.

Old Repela recited the ballad for a second time, and everyone considered his tale in the light of that ingenuous criticism and found nothing to object to, that is to say they granted it all the necessary licence.

*

As the years have passed, we have heard many and most diverse versions of that same adventure of *The Miller and the*

Magistrate's Wife, always from the lips of village and farmyard jesters in the mould of the now deceased Repela, and we have read it moreover in print in different collections of *Blindmen's Ballads*, or even in the famous *Ballads* collected by the unforgettable Don Agustín Durán.

The heart of the matter is always the same: tragicomic, spicy and abundantly epigrammatic, like all the moralising dramatic lessons Spanish people are so fond of; but the form, the chain of coincidences, the chance encounters, differ enormously from our shepherd's tale, so much so that he could never have recited any of these versions down on the farm, or any of those that are in print until the chaste girls had covered their ears or run the risk their mothers would give them a drubbing. Gross bumpkins from other provinces have bent and perverted to such an extent the traditional tale that was so delicious, delightful and discreet on the lips of the canonical Repela!

For a long time we have wanted to reassert the truth of things and restore the original character of that striking story, which we never doubted was the one which kept decorum intact. For, make no mistake about it, this kind of narrative, let loose in the hands of the common people, is never transformed into something more beautiful, delicate and decent, but is always tarnished and deformed by contact with the obscene and vulgar.

So much for the history of the present book... Let's dirty our own hands now – I mean begin – *The Magistrate and the Miller's Wife*, and hope, dear Reader, that 'after you've read it and crossed yourself more times than if you'd seen the devil', as the picaresque Estebanillo González once put it when starting to tell his own tale, 'your good sense deems it worthy of having seen the light of day'.

– July 1874

1

About when it happened

This lengthy century, now dying a death, had just begun. Nobody knows the exact year; we only know for certain it was after 1804 and before 1808.

Don Carlos IV of Bourbon still ruled over Spain, 'by the grace of God', according to the coins of the realm, and by the special grace or forgetfulness of Napoleon Bonaparte, according to the French gazetteers. All Louis XIV's other European descendants had already lost their crowns (and the headman, his head) in the storms which ravaged this rickety part of the world after 1789.

And it wasn't the only idiosyncrasy of our beloved Spain in those distant days. The Soldier of the Revolution, son of an obscure Corsican lawyer, all conquering in Rivoli, the pyramids, Marengo and a hundred battles more, had recently donned the crown of Charlemagne and totally transfigured Europe, creating and suppressing nations, erasing frontiers, inventing dynasties and changing the shape, name, place, customs and even clothes of the peoples wherever he rode his stallion of war, like an active earthquake, or the 'Antichrist' as the Northern European powers called him… Nevertheless, far from hating or fearing him, our forebears (may God preserve them in his Holy Glory), fairly revelled in the contemplation of his unlikely deeds, as if he were the hero of a chivalresque romance, or as if such things happened on another planet, with never the hint of a suspicion that he might ever venture their way to enact the atrocities he had inflicted on France, Italy, Germany and further afield. Once a week (twice at most) the mail from Madrid reached most important towns on

7

the peninsula, bringing the occasional issue of the *Gazette* (it wasn't daily anyway), and thus pre-eminent personages (supposing the *Gazette* reported the episode) learnt how one state more or less now existed beyond the Pyrenees, how another battle had been unleashed in which six or eight kings and emperors were embroiled, and whether Napoleon was in Milan, Brussels or Warsaw… Otherwise, our elders still lived in the antique Spanish style, extremely slowly, clinging to their rancid customs, to the peace and grace of God, to their Inquisition and friars, their quaint inequalities before the law, their personal privileges, rights and exemptions, their total lack of municipal or political freedoms, simultaneously governed by distinguished bishops and powerful magistrates (whose respective areas of power were not easily defined, since they both intervened in matters temporal and eternal), and paying tithes, first fruit, dues royal and ecclesiastical, income tax, inheritance tax, poll tax, purchase tax, window tax, compulsory alms… and over fifty tributes more, the nomenclature of which we can ignore for the moment.

And so concludes any connection the present story might have with the military and political affairs of that era; for we have only noted what was then happening in the world in order to point out that in the year in question (let's imagine it was 1805) the *ancien régime* ruled over every sphere of public and private life, and that, as if affronted by so much novelty and upheaval, the Pyrenees had become a second Great Wall of China.

2

The way people lived then

In Andalusia, for example (and what you are about to hear did in fact take place in Andalusia), people of standing still rose at the crack of dawn; went to early-morning Mass at the cathedral, even though it wasn't obligatory; breakfasted at nine on a fried egg with a cup of hot chocolate and fried bread; from one to two ate thick broth and a main course, if there were game and, if not, broth alone; had a siesta after lunch; then took a walk in the country; went to tell their rosaries for the Virgin Mary at twilight in their respective parish churches; had more chocolate at evensong (this time with sugary sponge fingers); the high and mighty attended the *conversazione* at the magistrate's, the dean's, or in the house of whichever entitled person resided in town; locked their front doors before the curfew tolled; supped on salad and stew par excellence, if fresh whitebait hadn't arrived, and immediately went to bed with their gentle ladies (those who had such), not without first having the bed warmed for nine months of the year…

Oh happy days when our land still cherished its quiet, peaceful possession of every cobweb, woodworm, shibboleth, belief, tradition, indeed every use and abuse hallowed down the centuries! Oh happy days when human society contrived a variety of classes, affections and customs! Oh happy days, I say, particularly for poets, who found an entr'acte, a skit, a comedy, a melodrama, an Everyman, or epic on every street corner, rather than the prosaic uniformity and insipid realism which the French Revolution finally bequeathed to us! Oh happy days!…

But let's not go round the houses again. Enough of generalities and circumlocutions, let's resolutely embark on our tale of *The Three-Cornered Hat*.

3

I give unto thee that thee may give unto me

In those days, then, there was near the city of *** a famous flour mill (that is no more), a quarter of a league from town, between a gentle hill planted with cherries, both ordinary and morello, and a most fertile orchard that acted as a bank (and sometimes as a bed) to an intermittent, treacherous and titular river.

For reasons various and diverse, that mill had long been a favourite destination and resting place for the finest promenaders from the aforesaid city... Firstly, it was served by a less unfriendly cart track than the rest in the region. Secondly, in front of the mill was a small flagstoned square, shaded by a huge grapevine, beneath which a wonderful cool was enjoyed in summer and sun in winter, thanks to the coming and going of the leaves... Thirdly, the miller was a very respectful, diplomatic, polite soul, who had the gift of the gab and flattered the lordly company which honoured him with their post-siesta chit-chat, by offering them whatever was in season, be it green beans, cherries, both ordinary and morello, undressed lettuces (delicious when accompanied by dumplings done in olive oil; dumplings our lordships took good care to send in advance), be it melons, grapes from the very vine which acted as an arbour, corn on the cob, if it was winter, and roasted chestnuts, almonds and walnuts, and occasionally, on frosty evenings, a round of mulled wine (now inside and by the fireside), to which at Easter he would add honey cakes, sugary tarts, buns or slices of ham from the Alpujarras.

Was the miller that rich, or his guests so profligate? you will interject.

Neither is the case. The miller managed to make ends meet, and those gentlemen were pride and prickliness personified. But in times when one paid fifty and more different taxes to Church and State, such a clear-sighted countryman risked little by winning the goodwill of councillors, canons, friars, town clerks and other highfalutin citizens. So there was no dearth of people who said old Lucas (for such was the miller's name) saved himself a packet each year by dint of entertaining *tout le monde*.

'Your good sir could give me a little old door from the house he has demolished,' he'd say to one. 'Your Most Worshipful (he'd say to another) can ask for a reduction in my income tax, or tithes or land tax.' 'Your Reverence will kindly let me pick some leaves from the convent garden for my silkworms.' 'Your Excellency will afford me a permission to gather wood from hill X'. 'The Most Reverend Father will pen two lines so I can cut wood in pine grove H.' 'I need Your Worship to write a deed that won't cost me a cent.' 'This year I can't pay the census.' 'I hope the case is decided in my favour.' 'Today I whacked someone, and I think he should be jailed for provoking me.' 'Has your good person got a spare such and such?' 'Do you really need that ?' 'Can you lend me a mule?' 'Is your cart being used tomorrow?' 'How about if I send for your donkey…'

And he would sing these tunes and always receive generous, disinterested responses: '*Whatever you need…*'

As you can see, old Lucas was not on the road to ruin.

4

A woman seen from the outside

The final, perhaps most powerful reason the city gentry had to flock to old Lucas' mill of an afternoon was that both clergy and laymen, from the bishop to the chief magistrate, could contemplate at leisure one of the most beautiful, gracious, wonderful works ever to emerge from the hands of the Almighty, then dubbed the *Supreme Being* by the enlightened politician Jovellanos and all the Francophiles in our country.

This masterpiece… went by the name of 'Señora Frasquita'.

I'll tell you first of all that Señora Frasquita, old Lucas' legitimate spouse, was a respectable lady, and all the mill's distinguished visitors knew that: none showed signs of eyeing her lustfully or sinfully. Of course, they admired her, and often paid her compliments (in front of her husband, naturally), whether friars, gentlemen, canons or town clerks, as a prodigious beauty who honoured her Creator, and a coquettish, mischievous imp who brought innocent cheer to the most melancholy of spirits. 'She's an exquisite animal,' proclaimed the very virtuous prelate. 'An ancient Hellenic statue,' observed an extremely erudite lawyer and corresponding member of the Academy of History. 'She's the spitting image of Eve,' exclaimed the Franciscan prior. 'She's a real dish,' declared the Colonel of the Militias. 'A serpent, a siren, a she-devil!' added the chief magistrate. 'But she's a good woman, an angel, a four-year-old child,' they all commented, returning from the mill stuffed on grapes or nuts, in search of their dismal, well-ordered hearths.

This little four-year old, namely, Señora Frasquita, must have been around the thirty mark.

She was a good five-foot six and appropriately sturdy, or perhaps stouter than her proud height warranted. She seemed a colossal Niobe[2], though she'd not borne children: nay, a female Hercules; nay, a Roman matron of the kind still stalking the Trastevere.

But it was her movement that was most striking – the agile, fluent grace of her fine form. She lacked the monumental repose to be the statue signalled by the academician. She swayed like a reed, gyrated like a weathervane, spun like a top. Her face was even more on the move, and, hence, less sculptural. As many as five dimples lent it wit and charm: one cheek with two; another with one; a minuscule item, by the left corner of her laughing lips, and in the middle of her round chin, the last, really large specimen. Add to this mix her mischievous grins and fetching winks and the varied poses of her head which spiced her conversation and you'll soon picture a face full of wit and beauty, ever radiating health and happiness.

Neither Señora Frasquita nor old Lucas was Andalusian: she was Navarrese and he was Murcian. He had gone to the city of *** as a fifteen-year-old half-page, half-servant to the previous bishop who had ruled that church. His protector brought him up to be a cleric, and perhaps to this end bequeathed him his mill so that he might enjoy some income; but when his most illustrious patron died, old Lucas had only taken minor orders and he hung up his habit at once to join the ranks, more eager to see the world and exciting adventures than sing Mass or grind grain. In 1793 he was part of the western Pyrenees campaign, an orderly to the valiant general Don Ventura Caro; he witnessed the assault on the Chateau Pignon, and then stayed on a long time in the northern provinces, where he finally left the forces. In Estella he met

Señora Frasquita, then known only as Frasquita; wooed her; married her; and took her off to Andalusia in search of the mill which was to give them so much peace and happiness in the rest of their pilgrimage through this valley of tears and laughter.

Transported from Navarra to such solitudes, Señora Frasquita had acquired no Andalusian customs, and was very different from the countrywomen of thereabouts. She dressed more simply, elegantly and naturally than they; washed more frequently, and allowed the sun and air to caress her bare arms and neck. Up to a point, she wore clothes in the style of the grand ladies of the day, as worn by Goya's[3] women, or by Queen María Luisa[4]: if not a very tight skirt, at least a shortish, fairly clinging skirt to display her dainty feet and the flourish of her regal legs. She wore her neckline low, Madrid fashion, a city where she spent two months with her Lucas on their journey from Navarra to Andalusia; she wore her hair gathered in a bun to show off her elegant head and neck, an earring in each tiny ear, and many rings on the slender fingers of her clean dexterous hands. Finally, Señora Frasquita's voice played the full range of tones of the most melodious instrument and her peals of laughter were so cheerful and silvery they sounded like church bells on Easter Sunday.

Let's now portray old Lucas.

5

A man seen from the outside and the in

Old Lucas was uglier than sin. And had been for his whole life of almost forty years. Nevertheless, God can have brought into the world few men as pleasant and agreeable. Captivated by his liveliness, wit and intelligence, the deceased bishop requested him from his parents: they were shepherds of real sheep, not of souls. After His Grace died and the lad had left the seminary for the barracks, General Caro singled him out from all his soldiers, and made him his closest orderly, his real aide-de-camp. When he'd finally done his military duty, old Lucas found it as easy to win the heart of Señora Frasquita as it had been to gain the approval of the general and the prelate. The Navarran, a sweet twenty at the time, and in the sights of all the lads in Estella, including the well heeled, couldn't resist the Murcian's constant joking, his lovesick monkey eyes and warm, perpetual smile that were both engaging and cheeky. The old soldier was so audacious and loquacious, so elegant and knowledgeable, so valiant and mirthful, that he finally won over the much sought-after beauty herself and even her father and mother.

At the time Lucas was, and continued to be at the time of our story, a man of small stature (at least relative to his wife), slightly round-shouldered, swarthy, smooth-cheeked, big-nosed, big-eared and pockmarked. On the other hand, his mouth was well formed and his teeth were without peer. One might say that only the man's bark was rough and ugly; that as soon as one penetrated to the inner man, his perfections appeared, and that his teeth were the beginning of such perfection. Next came his voice, vibrant, elastic, attractive;

sometimes manly and serious, sometimes sweet and honeyed when he asked for something, and always difficult to resist. Then there was what his voice said: ever opportune, discreet, witty, persuasive… And finally, old Lucas' soul possessed courage, loyalty, honesty, common sense, a desire to learn, and an instinctive or empirical knowledge of many things, a profound contempt for fools, whatever their social class, and an ironic, mocking, sarcastic spirit which made the academician dub him an unvarnished version of our Golden-Age writer, Don Francisco de Quevedo[5].

Such was old Lucas on the outside and the in.

6

A talented couple

Señora Frasquita was consequently madly in love with old Lucas and thought herself the happiest woman in the world because he adored her. They had no children, as we've mentioned, and concentrated on caring and looking after one another in every possible detail, but their tender loving care never manifested the cloying, sentimental character usually associated with almost all childless marriages because of the self-indulgence they generate. On the contrary, they behaved straightforwardly, cheerfully, with trusting good humour, like children who play and have fun together, who love one another with all their heart without saying a word – or ever realising what they feel.

In no way could there be on this earth a better groomed, dressed or fed miller, surrounded by more domestic conveniences than old Lucas! In no way could any miller's wife or queen have been the object of so much affection, so many attentions or kind thoughts as Señora Frasquita! In no way indeed could any mill have contained so many necessary, useful, agreeable, playful or even superfluous things as the one which provides the scenario for almost all the present story!

It very much helped that Señora Frasquita, that well-dressed, hard-working, strong, healthy Navarrese woman, knew how to, wanted, and was able to cook, sew, embroider, bake cakes, wash, iron, whitewash the house, wash the dishes, knead, weave, knit, sing, dance, play the guitar and castanets, a good hand of cards, and many other things too numerous to list. And it didn't help any less that old Lucas knew how to, wanted, and was able to organise the milling, sow the fields, hunt, fish, work as carpenter, blacksmith and bricklayer, support his wife in all the household chores, read, write, count, etc., etc. Not to mention his luscious plants, his most extravagant gifts.

For example, old Lucas adored flowers (as did his wife), and was such an artful horticulturist that he succeeding in producing new species through laborious grafting. He was something of a natural engineer, which he demonstrated by constructing a dam, a pump and an aqueduct that trebled the mill's water supply. He'd taught a dog to dance, tamed a snake, and trained a parrot to squawk the time as marked on a sundial the miller had drawn on a wall; consequently the parrot told the time to the minute, even on cloudy days and at night.

Finally, the mill had a garden which produced all manner of fruit and vegetables; a pond enclosed in a jasmine bower, where old Lucas and Señora Frasquita swam in summer; a garden; a greenhouse or conservatory for exotic plants; a fountain of drinking water; two donkeys the couple rode into the city or neighbouring villages; a chicken coop, dovecote, aviary, fish farm, silkworm farm; beehives, the bees of which feasted on the jasmine; a winepress, with its corresponding cellar, each in miniature; a baking oven, a loom, an anvil, a carpenter's workshop etc., etc., all fitted into an eight-roomed house and two fanegas of land, with an estimated value of ten thousand *reales*.

7

The heights of happiness

So the miller and his wife were madly in love, and one might even have thought she loved him more than he did her, though he was so ugly and she so beautiful. I say this because Señora Frasquita was jealous and wanted to know why old Lucas arrived very late from the city or villages where he went for grain, while old Lucas would look with pleasure on the attentions Señora Frasquita received from gentlemen who visited the mill; he was proud and delighted that she pleased them as much as she pleased him and, though he understood the envy some harboured in the bottom of their hearts and how they desired her as simple mortals and would have given the world for her not to be a respectable woman, he left her alone for days on end, and never asked her what she'd done or who'd been there in his absence...

That didn't at all mean that old Lucas' love was any less fervent than Señora Frasquita's. He merely trusted her virtue more than she did his; his insight was merely more profound, and he knew how much she loved him and how much self-respect his wife had; fundamentally old Lucas was every inch a man: a man like Shakespeare's, of few and indivisible sentiments; incapable of doubt; who believed or died; who lived or killed; who did not admit shades or slippage between supreme happiness and the destruction of bliss.

He was, in a word, an Othello from Murcia, with open-toed sandals and saddle, in the first act of a possible tragedy...

But why these melancholy notes in such a happy melody? Why this ominous lightning in such tranquillity? Why these melodramatic attitudes in such a bucolic scene?

You are about to find out right now.

8

The man in the three-cornered hat

It was two o'clock on an October afternoon.

The main cathedral bell was ringing for vespers, which meant that every pillar of society had eaten.

Canons headed to their choir stalls, and lay folk to their bedrooms to sleep the siesta, particularly those who, through their status – for example, the powers-that-be – had toiled the whole morning long.

It was very odd then that – at such an inappropriate hour for promenading, since it was still too hot – followed by a single constable, the illustrious magistrate of the aforesaid city should be setting forth on foot, a man who could not be mistaken for any other, by day or night, because of the huge size of his three-cornered hat, the gaudiness of his purple cloak and most peculiar nature of his grotesque gait...

Many people are still alive who could speak with personal knowledge of his purple cloak and three-cornered hat. We include ourselves in their number, with all those born in that city in the last days of the reign of Don Fernando VII, who remember seeing hanging from a nail – the single adornment of a dilapidated wall, in the dilapidated tower to the house His Honour inhabited – the two antiquated garments, a hat and a cloak – black hat on top, red cloak beneath – a sort of spectre of Absolutism, a sort of shroud for the magistrate, a sort of retrospective caricature of his power, painted in charcoal and red ochre, like so many others, by the 'constitutional youngsters' of 1837 who gathered there; in other words, a kind of scarecrow who, at other times, had been a scareman, youths who today, I'm afraid, add insult to injury by stalking him around that historic city on carnival days, strung up on a chimneysweep's stick, or acting as a derisory disguise for the fool who most made the populace laugh… A pathetic principle of authority! That's how we set you up, we who invoke you so much today!

As for the magistrate's grotesque gait, which we've mentioned, it consisted (so they say) in his being round-shouldered… even more round-shouldered than old Lucas… almost hunchbacked, to put it crudely; of less than average height; weedy; in bad health; bow-legged with a very sui generis way of walking (swaying from one side to another and backwards and forwards) that can only be described by the absurd formulation of his apparently possessing two lame feet. On the other hand (so tradition has it), his face was ordinary, though hugely wrinkled by a total absence of teeth and molars; biliously swarthy, like most sons of the two Castiles; he had large dark eyes, where flashed anger, despotism and lust; malevolent, scheming traits that aired not personal courage but artful malice capable of anything, and a touch of half-aristocratic, half-libertine self-satisfaction which revealed how, in his distant youth, the fellow had been a great success with the women, despite his legs and hump.

Don Eugenio de Zuñiga y Ponce de León (for such was His Honour's name) had been born in Madrid, into a distinguished family; he was now some fifty-five years old and had been magistrate for four in the city that concerns us, where, just after his arrival, he married the most pre-eminent lady, to whom we shall return later.

Don Eugenio's stockings (the only apparel, apart from his shoes, which his huge purple cloak enabled one to see) were white and his shoes black and gold-buckled. But the moment the heat of the countryside forced him to shed his cloak, one saw his big cotton tie; dove-coloured serge waistcoat festooned with green posies embroidered in filigree; short, black-silk breeches; a huge frock coat of the same stuff as his waistcoat; a steel-hilted dress sword; a tasselled walking stick; and a fine pair of straw-coloured chamois gloves (or gauntlets) that he never wore but grasped like a sceptre.

Twenty steps behind the magistrate followed the constable, called Ferret, who lived up to his name. Skinny and nimble; looking forward and back, left and right at the same time as he walked; long-necked; a tiny, repugnant face, with hands like two cat-o'-nine-tails, he seemed a beadle in search of criminals, the rope to tie them up, and the chosen instrument of punishment.

The first magistrate who clapped eyes on him said without more ado: '*You will be my top constable…*', and he'd already seen off four magistrates.

He was forty-eight, and wore a much smaller three-cornered hat than his master (for, we insist, his was outlandish), a cloak as black as his stockings, his whole garb, stick and a kind of spit which served as a sword.

This black scarecrow was like the shadow of his gaudy master.

9

Get along, donkey!

Wherever this character and his appendage promenaded, the farmers abandoned their hoes and bowed reverentially to their toes, more out of fear than respect, and then whispered:

'The magistrate's off early in the afternoon to see the miller!'

'Early… and all alone!' some added, used to seeing him stroll that way in considerable company.

'Hey, Manuel: how come His Honour is going to see the Navarrese woman by himself this afternoon?' a peasant woman asked her husband who was transporting her on the back of his beast of burden.

And with that, she tickled him knowingly.

'Don't be so wicked, Josefa!' the good man exclaimed. 'Señora Frasquita would never…'

'Too right… But that doesn't mean the magistrate isn't in love with her… I've heard that, of all them who go partying at the mill, the fellow from Madrid, so fond of a little bit of skirt, is the only man intent on evil…'

'And how come you know he is or isn't fond of a little bit of skirt?' asked her husband in turn.

'I wouldn't know myself… He may be a magistrate and all that, but he'd know better than to praise my beautiful black eyes!'

The one who spoke thus was ugly in the extreme.

'Well, my dear, that's their affair!' replied the man called Manuel. 'I can't see old Lucas agreeing… He's got a terrible temper when he gets angry!…'

'But, if he thinks it's of use!…' snorted old Josefa.

'Old Lucas is a respectable fellow…' the countryman

replied, 'and a respectable man can never think such things of use…'

'Well, you're right then. It's their affair! If I were Señora Frasquita!…'

'Get along, donkey!' her husband shouted, changing the subject.

And the jenny trotted off, taking the rest of their conversation with her.

10

Up the vine

While the countryfolk bantered as they greeted the magistrate, Señora Frasquita carefully washed and swept the flagstoned square that served as an atrium or centre to the mill, and set out half a dozen chairs under the thickest part of the vine, where old Lucas had climbed to cut the ripest bunches, which he was now arranging artistically in a basket.

'Well, you're right, Frasquita!' said old Lucas from the top of the vine. 'The magistrate is in love with you and in a bad way…'

'I told you so a long time ago,' retorted his northern wife, '… but let him sweat! Take care, Lucas, don't fall!'

'Don't worry, I've got a good grip… You also quite fancy him…'

'Don't be silly! Tell me something I don't know!' she interrupted. 'You don't have to tell me who fancies me and who doesn't! And pray tell me why you don't fancy me!'

'Easy! Because you're so ugly…' old Lucas answered.

'Well… Ugly I might be, but I can soon get up that vine and knock you off your perch!…'

'No, you can't, for I'd most likely not let you back down till I'd eaten you alive…'

'Too true!… And when my gallants get here, they'd say we were a couple of monkeys!'

'And they'd be right, because you're a right pretty little monkey and I'm a monkey that's got a hump…'

'Which I like a lot…'

'Then you must prefer the magistrate's, as his is bigger than mine…'

'Come, come! Don Lucas… Don't be so jealous!…'

'Me? Jealous of that old soak? Quite the contrary; I'm very happy he loves you!…'

'Why?'

'Because sin leads to penitence. You will never love him, and in the meantime I'm the city's real magistrate!'

'Who's a Señor Modest! Well, as for loving me… Stranger things have been known!…'

'It wouldn't upset me too greatly…'

'Why?'

'Because then you wouldn't be yourself; and, not being your true self or the one I believe you to be, damned if I'd care if the devil ran off with you!'

'Well, what would you do in such a situation?'

'Me? How do I know!… Because in that case I'd be someone else and not the man I am now and can't imagine what I might think…'

'And why would you turn into someone else?' Señora Frasquita persisted valiantly, as she stopped sweeping, put her hands on her hips and looked up.

Old Lucas scratched his head, as if scratching around for a very profound idea, until finally he declared more gravely and elegantly than was his wont:

'I'd be someone else because now I'm a man who believes in you as in himself and lives only through that faith. So, if that belief died, I too would die or turn into a new man. I'd live differently; I'd think I'd just been born; I'd have other feelings. I don't know what I'd do with you... I might laugh and turn my back on you... I might not even recognise you... I might... But how we enjoy putting ourselves in a bad mood for no reason at all! What could we care if all the world's magistrates loved you? Aren't you my very own Frasquita?'

'Yes, you rascal you!' retorted the Navarran, laughing fit to burst. 'I'm your Frasquita, and you're my lovely Lucas, uglier than a scarecrow, the cleverest man alive, more honest and loved than a loaf of bread... And as for fancying you, you just wait till you get down from that vine! You'll be more pinched and slapped than you've got hairs on your head! But, shush! What can I see now! The magistrate approaching completely alone... And so early!... He's up to no good...'

'Well, steel yourself, and don't tell him I'm up the vine. He's come all by himself to declare his love to you. He reckons he'll catch me sleeping the siesta! I'll have a good laugh listening to him explaining himself.'

And that was what old Lucas said as he handed the basket down to his wife.

'Don't be so wicked!' she exclaimed, laughing even more loudly. 'The devil take this fellow from Madrid! Does he think he's a magistrate made for me? But here he is already... And Ferret bringing up the rear, sitting on the path in the shade!... What knaves! Hide behind the vine leaves. We'll have more fun than you can imagine...'

And, after saying this, the beautiful Navarran started to sing a fandango that was now as familiar to her as the songs of her own land.

Pamplona under siege

'God protect you, Frasquita…' mumbled the magistrate, tiptoeing into view beneath the vine.

'How nice to see you, chief magistrate!' she responded quite naturally, dropping him a thousand curtsies. 'Your Honour here at this time of day! And in this heat! Come and be seated, Your Honour! It's so cool here. Why didn't Your Honour wait for the other gentlemen? I've already set out their seats… This afternoon we're expecting the bishop in person, for he promised my Lucas he'd come to taste the first grapes from the vine. And how is Your Honour? And Her Ladyship?'

The magistrate looked embarrassed. Frasquita's blessed solitude seemed like a dream, or a trap laid by hostile fortune to make him plunge down an abyss of disappointment.

So his only answer was: 'It's not as early as you say, my dear. It must be at least half-past three…'

The parrot squawked right on cue.

'It's a quarter-past two,' said the Navarrese woman, looking the man from Madrid right in the eyes.

He went silent, like a convicted criminal refusing to defend himself.

'What about Lucas? Is he asleep?' he asked after a while.

(We should point out that the magistrate, like all toothless people, spoke with a sibilant lisp, as if munching his own teeth.)

'Of course!' answered Señora Frasquita. 'At this time of day he nods off wherever it catches him, even on the edge of an abyss…'

'Well, let him sleep on!' the old magistrate exclaimed,

turning a deeper shade of pale. 'And you, my lovely Frasquita, listen to me… Come here… Sit by my side! I've got so much to tell you…'

'No sooner said than done,' replied the miller's wife, grabbing a low chair and planting it down in front of the magistrate's nose.

As soon as she'd sat down, Frasquita crossed her legs, leant forward, rested one elbow on her knee, and her mischievous, beautiful face on her hand; and thus, her head to one side, her lips a-smiling, her five dimples on active service, staring serenely at the magistrate, she waited for His Honour to declare himself. Like Pamplona waiting to be bombed by Old Boney.

The poor fellow made as if to speak, his mouth lolling open, enraptured by that formidable woman's grandiose beauty and graceful splendour, her alabaster, opulent flesh, her fresh, smiling lips, her blue, bottomless eyes, all as if painted by Ruben's brush.

'Frasquita!' His Majesty's representative sighed and swooned, while his pallid, sweaty face, silhouetted against his hump, exuded deep anguish: 'Frasquita!'

'That's my name!' answered the daughter of the Pyrenees. 'What, prithee?'

'Whatever you crave…' replied the old man ever so tenderly.

'Well, what I want…' replied the miller's wife, 'Your Honour knows only too well. I want Your Honour to appoint a nephew of mine from Estella as secretary to the town council… so he can depart those mountains where he's having a really bad time…'

'I've told you, dear Frasquita, how that's impossible. The present secretary…'

'Is a thieving, drunken animal!'

'I know… But he's got influence over the unelected councillors and I can't appoint another without the council's agreement. Otherwise, I risk…'

'I risk!… I risk!… What wouldn't Your Honour risk for the kitties of this house!'

'Is that the price of love, my darling?' stammered the magistrate.

'No, sir: for I want Your Worship for nothing.'

'Dear, forget the titles! Look me in the eye, be as familiar as you like… So you'll love me, won't you? Tell me, my dear.'

'Didn't I say I wanted it now?'

'But…'

'No buts about it. You'll see what a handsome, honest fellow my nephew is!'

'You're so pretty, my Frascuela!…'

'Do you fancy me?'

'Do I fancy you?… You're my one and only!'

'Well, take a close look… Nothing's fake here…' responded Señora Frasquita, rolling up her blouse sleeve to show the magistrate the whole of an arm, worthy of a caryatid and whiter than an Easter lily.

'Do I fancy you!…' continued His Honour. 'By night, by day, at every hour, and everywhere, I think only of you!'

'Oh, really. Don't you like Her Ladyship?' enquired Señora Frasquita with an ill-feigned compassion that would have had a hypochondriac in fits of laughter. 'What a pity! My Lucas told me he had the pleasure of meeting and talking with her when he went to set right your bedroom clock, and that she's very beautiful, very pleasant and extremely affectionate.'

'I wouldn't go that far!' muttered the magistrate rather sourly.

'On the other hand, some people have told me,' the miller's wife went on, 'she's very irritable, very jealous and that you shake more than a willow in the wind…'

'I wouldn't go that far!…' repeated Don Eugenio de Zuñiga y Ponce de León, blushing a crimson red, 'either one way or the other! My good lady does have her moods, it's true… but as for making me shake, that's going too far. I am the chief magistrate!'

'But, tell me, do you love her, yes or no?'

'I can tell you… I love her dearly… or did so before I met you. But from the moment I saw you, I don't know what hit me, and she knows something's up… By way of example, I can tell you that touching her face is like feeling my own… You see, I couldn't love her more, yet feel less!… Whereas to touch your hand, your arm, your face, your waist, I'd give what is not mine to give!'

And, blathering thus, the magistrate snatched at the naked arm Señora Frasquita was literally rubbing in his eyes; she kept a straight face, however, and stretched out a hand, tapped His Honour on the chest in a peacefully violent move, with the unmatched might of an elephant's trunk, and over he went, chair and all.

'Jesus, Joseph and Mary!' the Navarran exclaimed, laughing her head off. 'That chair must have been broken…'

'What's up down there?' shouted old Lucas, his ugly face peering out from amid the green shoots of the vine.

The magistrate was still flat on his back, eyeing with unspeakable terror that man who had appeared mid-air and was looking down on him.

One might have said His Honour was the devil, defeated not by St Michael, but by another devil from hell.

'What's happened down here?' Señora Frasquita replied,

flustered. 'Well, His Honour leant back in his chair, started to rock, then fell over!...'

'Jesus, Mary and Joseph!' the miller exclaimed in turn. 'And has His Honour hurt himself? Would you like a splash of vinegar and water?'

'I'm as right as rain!' shouted the magistrate, pulling himself up as best he could.

And then he whispered, so only Señora Frasquita could hear him:

'You'll both pay for this!...'

'On the other hand, Your Honour saved my life,' retorted old Lucas, not shifting from the top of the vine. 'Just imagine, my love, here I sat contemplating the grapes, when I nodded off on a tangle of branches and sticks that left enough gaps for my body to fall right through... So if Your Honour's fall hadn't woken me up in time, I'd have broken my skull on the flagstones...'

'In that case...' retorted the magistrate, 'I'm really pleased for your sake... I can tell you how glad I am I fell over!

'You'll pay for this!' he added, staring at the miller's wife.

And he pronounced those words with such a look of concentrated fury that Señora Frasquita felt really apprehensive.

She could see clearly how the magistrate had taken fright first, thinking the miller had heard everything; but convinced he'd heard nothing (for old Lucas' calm dissimulation would have deceived the most eagle-eyed), he'd begun to surrender to his ire and plot his revenge.

'Come on! Get down from there and help me clean His Honour up, for he could do with a real dusting!' the miller's wife then shouted.

And as the miller climbed down, she told the magistrate, as

she hit him on the face, and occasionally on the ears, with her apron:

'The poor man didn't hear a thing... He was sleeping like a log...'

More than the words themselves, the fact they were whispered, implying complicity and secrecy, wrought a magic effect.

'You wicked scoundrel!' stammered Don Eugenio de Zuñiga, his mouth watering, still grumbling...

'Do you still bear me a grudge?' simpered the Navarran.

As the magistrate now saw how severity paid good dividends, he tried to look at Señora Frasquita really angrily, but he met her tempting laugh and divine eyes, where there was a hint of supplication, and he turned sentimental on the spot, lisped sibilantly, displayed more than ever his total lack of teeth and molars:

'That's down to you, my love!'

At that very moment old Lucas swung down from the vine.

12

Of tithes and first fruit

The magistrate was restored to his chair and the miller's wife glanced at her husband, whom she found as placid as ever and stifling a desire to laugh at the incident; taking advantage of His Honour's first lapse of concentration, she blew him a kiss from afar, and finally spoke to Don Eugenio in siren tones Cleopatra would have envied:

'Now Your Lordship can taste my grapes!'

You should have seen the beautiful Navarran (and I'd

paint her if I had Titian's brush), posing before the infatuated magistrate, fresh as a rose, magnificent, her tall, noble figure sheathed in a tight dress, her naked arms raised above her head, a bunch of translucent grapes in each hand, combining an irresistible smile with a pleading look titillated by fear, as she entreated him:

'The bishop has yet to taste them… They are the first to be harvested this year…'

She was a huge Pomona[6] offering fruits to a peasant god; to a satyr, for instance.

At this the venerable bishop of the dioceses appeared at the far end of the flagstoned square, accompanied by the lawyer academician, two elderly canons, and his retinue of secretary, two familiars and two pages.

His Excellency stopped a moment to contemplate a scene at once comic and beautiful, until he finally declared in that monotonous accent proper in the prelates of the time:

'*On the fifth, payment of tithes and first fruit to the Church of God*, so teaches us Christian doctrine, but you, Señor Magistrate, not satisfied with administering the tithe, also want to eat the first fruit.'

'The bishop!' exclaimed the miller and his spouse, leaving the magistrate and running to kiss the prelate's ring.

'God reward Your Excellency for coming to honour our humble cottage!' intoned old Lucas reverentially, giving the first kiss.

'What a handsome bishop I have!' proclaimed Frasquita, kissing second. 'God bless and keep him more years than he has preserved my Lucas!'

'I don't know why you need me when you bless me rather than asking me to bless you!' laughed the good shepherd.

And extending two fingers, he blessed Señora Frasquita

and then the others gathered round.

'Here is the *first fruit*, Your Excellency!' said the magistrate, taking a bunch from the hands of the miller's wife and presenting them courteously to the bishop. 'I've yet to taste the grapes…'

The magistrate pronounced these words, glancing cynically in the direction of the miller's wife and her splendorous beauty…

'Well, it's not because they're unripe, like those in the fable!' observed the academician.

'Those in the fable,' added the bishop, 'weren't green, my learned friend, but beyond the vixen's reach.'

Neither probably alluded intentionally to the magistrate; but both sentences happened to fit perfectly the recent scene, so Don Eugenio turned purple and, kissing the prelate's ring, said:

'That, Your Excellency, is tantamount to calling me a fox!'

'You said it!' came the affably severe reply of a saint, as people said he in fact was. '*Excusatio non petita, accusatio manifesta.*[7] The style's the man. But *satis iam dictum, nullius ultra sit sermo.*[8] Or what comes to the same thing, let's forget our Latin and take a peek at these famous grapes.'

And he took a bite… only one… from the bunch presented by the magistrate.

'So sweet!' he exclaimed, holding his grape to the light before passing it quickly to his secretary. 'Pity they make me sick!'

The secretary also contemplated the grape; gestured politely and handed it on to one of the familiars.

The familiar repeated the bishop's action and the secretary's, dared even to sniff the grape, and then… placed it carefully in the basket, ensuring he whispered to the congregation: 'His Excellency is fasting...'

Old Lucas, whose eyes had followed the grape, took it on the sly and ate it without anyone noticing.

This done, they all sat down: they spoke of autumn (which was still very dry, though the fiestas of San Francisco had come and gone); debated the probability of a fresh outbreak of war between Napoleon and Austria; persisted in the belief that the imperial troops would never invade Spanish territory; the lawyer lamented the calamitous turbulence of the times, envied the tranquil era of his parents (as his parents must have envied their grandparents'); the parrot struck five... and, at a sign from the reverend bishop, the younger of the pages went to the episcopal carriage (that had stayed on the path with the constable), and returned with a magnificent cake baked in olive oil, dusted with salt, that had only left the oven an hour before: a table was set in their midst; the cake sliced; each given their share, despite old Lucas' and Señora Frasquita's vigorous protests... and a genuine democratic equality reigned for half an hour beneath vine shoots and leaves which filtered the final glimmers of a setting sun...

13

The kettle calls the pot black

An hour and a half later all the distinguished picnickers were back in the city.

The bishop and his 'family' had arrived quite early, thanks to their carriage, and were already in the 'palace' where we shall leave them to their devotions.

The learned lawyer (a dry stick) and the two canons (pillars of respectability) accompanied the magistrate to the door of the town hall (where His Honour said he had work to do), and then headed to their respective homes, guided by the stars like sailors or like blind men flailing on street corners; for night had closed in, the moon was not yet out, and street lighting (like this century's other lights) still resided in the mind of the Divinity.

On the other hand, it wasn't rare to see the odd torch or lantern wandering along a street when a respectful servant lit the path for his magnificent masters on their way to ritual *conversazione* or a visit to a relative's house…

Near all the wrought-iron grilles, one could see (or rather smell) a silent black hulk. Gallants who, on hearing footsteps, left their courting for a moment…

'We are a trio of rascals!' chorused the lawyer and the canons. 'What will they think in our homes when we arrive so late?'

'Well, what will people say who meet us in the street, like this, at past seven at night, like bandits lurking in the dark?'

'We must behave better…'

'Yes, but that lovely mill…'

'My wife feels it in the pit of her stomach…' said the academician, in a tone that revealed his terror at the approaching matrimonial dust-up.

'What about my niece?' exclaimed one of the canons, who was surely in charge of penances. 'My niece says priests shouldn't visit women of…'

'And yet,' interrupted his companion, who was chaplain-in-chief, 'what happens there is innocence itself…'

'Of course! Even the bishop goes!'

'And besides, gentlemen, at our age,' added the director of penances. 'I was seventy-five yesterday.'

'Of course!' replied the chaplain. 'But let's speak of more pleasant things: wasn't Señora Frasquita looking beautiful this afternoon!'

'Oh, yes, she's what you call really beautiful!' said the lawyer, attempting to be impartial.

'Very pretty...' responded the head of penance from inside the hood of his cloak.

'And if you are in doubt,' added the priest who officiated at Mass, 'just ask the chief magistrate.'

'The poor fellow's in love with her if you ask me!' exclaimed the cathedral's chief confessor.

'Too true!' added the correspondent to the Academy. 'So, good sirs, I go this way home... A very good night to you!'

'Goodnight...' answered the cathedral clergy.

They walked a few steps in silence.

'That man also fancies the miller's wife!' the chief chaplain murmured, digging the director of penances in the ribs with his elbow.

'And how!...' the latter replied, stopping before his front door. 'He's so unsubtle! See you tomorrow, my friend. Hope the grapes go down well.'

'See you tomorrow, God willing... Have a very good night.'

'May God grant us a good night!' prayed the director of penances, on his doorstep, that also possessed a lantern and a Virgin.

And he rapped on the door knocker.

Now alone in the street, the other canon (who was more broad than tall, and seemed more to roll than to walk) made his way slowly towards his house; but before arriving, he committed a certain affront against a wall that in the future would be the object of a police edict, and said, so doing, no doubt thinking of his brothers in the choir stalls:

'You also like Señora Frasquita!… And to tell the truth,' he added a moment later, 'she is what you call really beautiful!'

14

Advice from Ferret

Meanwhile, the magistrate had gone to the town hall accompanied by Ferret, and had been in the sessions room for a long time, deep in a conversation with him which was more personal than befitted his rank and trade.

'Your Honour should trust a gun dog who knows the hunt!' cried the shameless constable. 'Señora Frasquita is madly in love with Your Honour, and everything Your Honour has just told me helps me see more clearly than that light…'

And he pointed to a big candle from Lucena, which barely lit an eighth part of the room.

'I'm not so sure as you, Ferret!' sighed Don Eugenio, languidly.

'Well, why not! And, if not, let's be frank. Your Honour's body – pardon me – has a blemish… Right?'

'Yes, indeed!' retorted the magistrate. 'But old Lucas has the blemish too. He's more hunchbacked than I am!'

'Much more! A great deal more! No comparison! But on the other hand (this was his point), Your Lordship's a good-looker… really handsome… whereas old Lucas is like that Sergeant Utrera who died of ugliness.'

The magistrate smiled presumptuously.

'Besides,' the constable continued, 'Señora Frasquita is

quite capable of jumping out of the window to get her nephew appointed…'

'So far, so much agreed! That appointment is my only hope!'

'Well, shoulder to the boulder, sir! I've already told you of my plan… You must execute it this very night!'

'I've told you often enough I need no advice from you!' clamoured Don Eugenio, suddenly remembering he was talking to an inferior.

'I thought Your Honour had just asked me for some,' stammered Ferret.

'Don't answer back!'

Ferret saluted.

'And so you were saying,' continued de Zuñiga, calming down again, 'it can all be arranged tonight? Well, I think it's a good idea. What the hell! This way I'll be rid of cruel uncertainty!'

Ferret stayed silent.

The magistrate went to his office and wrote a few lines on a sheet of paper that bore a seal, which he sealed and put in his pocket.

'Her nephew's appointment is ready!' he exclaimed, taking a pinch of snuff. 'Tomorrow I'll settle it with the councillors… and they'll ratify it or there'll be hell to pay! Am I on the right road?'

'Oh, yes! Yes!' squealed Ferret enthusiastically, putting a paw in the magistrate's box and helping himself to a pinch. 'Yes! Yes! Your Honour's predecessor didn't do things by halves either. Once…'

'Stop the idle chit-chat!' retorted the magistrate, rapping the thieving hand. 'My predecessor was an idiot when he had you as a constable. But let's keep to what's our priority…

You just told me old Lucas' mill stands within the legal boundaries of the next village and not this town's... Do you swear to that?'

'A hundred per cent! The city's jurisdiction finishes at the path where I sat and waited for Your Lordship this afternoon... I swear to Old Nick! If I'd been in your shoes!...'

'Shut up!' shouted Don Eugenio. 'You're so rude!'

And he wrote a message on a half-sheet of paper, folded it, turned over the corner, and handed it to Ferret.

'There you are,' he told him as he did so, 'the letter you asked me to write to the village mayor. Spell out to him plainly everything he has to do. You see how I'm following your plan to the letter! Woe betide you if you send me down a blind alley!'

'Don't worry!' responded Ferret. 'Juan López has a lot to lose, and as soon as he sees Your Honour's signature, he'll do everything I tell him. He owes at least a thousand fanegas of wheat to the Royal Granary, and as much to the Granary for Charitable Works. He's totally broken the law, since he's no widow or poor labourer to get wheat without paying his dues and charges, but a gambling, drunken, womanising good-for-nothing who has scandalised his little hamlet... And the fellow is wielding authority!... What a state our world is in!'

'I told you to shut up! You're distracting me!' bawled the magistrate. 'Let's review tonight's plan,' he added, changing his tone. 'It's a quarter-past seven... First of all, you must go home and inform Her Ladyship not to expect me for supper or bed. Tell her I'll be here till curfew, and then I'm going on a secret patrol with you to see if we can't catch some miscreants... In a word, spin her a yarn so she goes to bed without a care in the world. While you're about it, tell another constable to bring me supper... I don't want to make an appearance before Her Ladyship tonight, for she knows me so well she can read my thoughts! Tell the cook to add some of those honey cakes they made today, and tell Juanete to send me half a litre of white wine from the tavern, and make sure nobody finds out. You go straight to the village and make sure you're there by half-past eight.'

'I'll be there at eight sharp!' Ferret exclaimed.

'Don't contradict me!' bellowed the magistrate remembering whom he was talking to yet again.

Ferret saluted him.

'We said,' he said, calming down again, 'you'll be there at eight sharp. It must be half a league from village to mill…'

'Hardly.'

'Don't interrupt!'

The constable saluted again.

'Hardly…' continued the magistrate. 'Right then, at ten o'clock… You reckon ten o'clock?…'

'Before ten! Your Honour can knock on the mill door at half-past nine without a care in the world!'

'Humph! Don't tell me what I must do! I expect you'll be…'

'Everywhere… But the path will be my base. Oh, I was forgetting… Go on foot and don't take a torch…'

'As if I damned well needed such advice! Do you think this is my first campaign?'

'Forgive me, Your Lordship… Oh, and also… Don't knock on the big door facing the flagstoned square, but the small door above the mill-race…'

'There's another door above the mill-race? Well, I'd certainly never have thought of that!'

'Yes, sir. The door over the mill-race leads straight into the bedroom of the miller and his wife… and old Lucas never uses it to go in or out. So even if he came back early…'

'I get you… Don't keep on!'

'Finally, Your Honour should scarper before dawn. Now sunrise is at six…'

'More pointless advice! I'll be back home by five… But that's enough talk… Be gone about your business!'

'Well, sir… good luck!' exclaimed the constable, holding a hand out towards the magistrate while looking up at the ceiling.

The magistrate dropped a peseta into his hand, and Ferret disappeared as if by magic.

'Egad!…' muttered the old man shortly. 'I forgot to tell that fellow to bring me a pack of cards! I'd have kept at it till half-past nine, seeing if the solitaire worked out for me!…'

15

A farewell in prose

It must have been nine o'clock that same evening by the time old Lucas and Señora Frasquita had finished their daily chores in the mill and house and could dine on a bowl of endives, a pound of meat cooked in tomato sauce, and a few of the grapes which remained in the aforesaid basket, all washed down with a drop of wine and great guffaws at the magistrate's expense: after which the couple glanced at each other, as if at peace with God and themselves, and said, with yawns that revealed the peace and tranquillity deep within their hearts:

'Well, my dear, let's go to bed, for tomorrow is another day.'

Just then they heard two loud knocks on their front door.

Husband and wife exchanged startled looks.

Never before had they heard knocking at their door so late in the night.

'I'll go and see...' said the intrepid Navarran, on her way to the little square.

'Don't you dare! This is my business!' exclaimed old Lucas so resonantly that Señora Frasquita made way for him. 'I told you to stay there!' he added gruffly, seeing his wife make as if to follow him.

She obeyed and stayed inside.

'Who goes there?' asked old Lucas from the middle of the square.

'The law!' a voice answered from beyond the thick door.

'What law?'

'The local kind. Open up for the mayor!'

In the meantime old Lucas had applied one eye to a peephole well hidden in the door, and in the moonlight recognised the rural mayor from the next village.

'You mean I should open up to a drunkard constable!' retorted the miller, sliding the bolt.

'It's yours truly!...' replied the man outside. 'I've got a summons written in His Honour's hand! A very good night to you, old Lucas...' he added much less officiously as he walked in.

'God keep you, Toñuelo,' replied the Murcian. 'Let's have a look at this summons of yours... And next time Juan López might choose a more opportune moment to apprehend an honest man! Of course, it's all your fault. Look at you, you've drunk your way through the orchards! Do you want a little drop more?'

'No, sir, there's no time for that. You must come with me at once. Read the summons.'

'What do you mean "come with you"?' exclaimed old

Lucas, going back into the mill, waving the paper. 'Come on, Frasquita, let's have some light!'

Señora Frasquita let go of something she was holding, and took down the candle.

Old Lucas took a quick look at the object his wife had dropped, and recognised his huge musket that fired half-pound shot.

His eyes filled with tender gratitude and he said to her, as he touched her face:

'You're a real jewel!'

Pale and serene like a marble statue, Señora Frasquita lifted up the candle between two fingers, her pulse not racing in the slightest, and responded drily:

'Come on, read it!'

The summons said:

> *In the greater service of H.M. the King Our Master (T.B.G.), I beseech Lucas Fernández, miller in this vicinity, to appear before my authority without any excuse or pretext to the contrary, as soon as receives the present summons; advising him that, as it is a reserved matter, he must inform nobody thereupon: in case of disobedience, all subject to the corresponding penalties. His Mayor,*
>
> *Juan López*

And there was a cross in place of a signature.

'Hey, you, what's this all about?' old Lucas quizzed the constable. 'What's this summons in aid of?'

'Not a clue…' replied the rustic policeman of thirty-odd years, whose twisted, cunning face, a thief, or a murderer's, pitifully reflected his sincerity. 'I think it's to do with witches, or fake money… But it's not to do with you… You're needed

as a witness or expert. Though nobody's told me the details…
Juan López will give you chapter and verse.'

'Got it!' shouted the miller. 'Tell him I'll come in the
morning.'

'No, no, sir!… You must come now, there's no time to lose.
They're my orders from the mayor.'

A moment's silence followed.

Señora Frasquita's eyes flashed angrily.

Old Lucas kept his glued to the ground, as if searching for
something.

'At least you'll give me enough time,' he finally exclaimed as
he looked up, 'to go to the stables and saddle my donkey…'

'What bloody donkey!' the constable retorted. 'Half a
league's not too far for any man! It's a beautiful night, the
moon's shining…'

'I had noticed it was out. But I've got swollen feet…'

'Well, there's no more time to waste. I'll help you saddle up
your donkey.'

'Hey, you mean you're afraid I might escape?'

'I'm afraid of nothing, old Lucas,' replied Toñuelo, as cold
as a fish. 'I am the law.'

And with those words, he stood at ease; and revealed the
half shotgun he was carrying under his cape.

'Well now, Toñuelo…' said the miller's wife. 'As you're
going to the stables… to exercise your proper trade… please
saddle the other donkey up for me.'

'Why?' asked the miller.

'For me! I'm coming with you.'

'You can't, Señora Frasquita!' the constable objected. 'I
have my orders to take only your husband, and to stop you
from following him. My neck and future depend on it. That's
what Juan López threatened. So, come on, old Lucas.'

And he headed for the door.

'How peculiar,' muttered the Murcian, rooted to the spot.

'How very, very peculiar!' echoed Señora Frasquita.

'There's something fishy… I can smell…' old Lucas kept muttering so Toñuelo couldn't hear.

'Do you want me to go to the city?' whispered the Navarran, 'and I'll tell the magistrate what's happened?'

'No!' bellowed old Lucas. 'No way!'

'Well, what should I do then?' demanded his wife forcefully.

'Look at me…' the old soldier replied.

Husband and wife looked silently at each other and, pleased by the calm, resolution and energy their souls communicated, they finally shrugged their shoulders and laughed.

Old Lucas then lit another candle and went off to the stable, jibing at Toñuelo as he walked towards him:

'Hey, you! Let's have some of that help you promised!'

Toñuelo followed him, humming a catchy tune.

A few minutes later old Lucas left the mill astride a beautiful jenny, with the constable trailing behind.

The couple's farewells were short and sweet.

'Lock up well…' said old Lucas.

'Wrap your cloak round your head, it's cold out there…' said Señora Frasquita, as she locked, bolted and barred the door.

And there were no more goodbyes, kisses, embraces or glances.

What was in store?

16

A bird of ill-omen

For our part, we will follow old Lucas.

The miller on his jenny and the constable prodding it on with his rod of state had already gone a quarter of a league in complete silence when they saw looming before them, at the point where the path twisted round a hill, the shadow of an enormous bird advancing towards them.

Lit by the moon, delineated clearly, the shadow stood out so emphatically the miller was forced to exclaim:

'Toñuelo, that's scrawny-legged Ferret in his three-cornered hat!'

But before he got an answer, the shadow, intent no doubt on avoiding the encounter, had left the path and started to run across the fields at a real ferret pace.

'I can't see anyone...' Toñuelo responded as naturally as you can imagine.

'Nor can I,' replied old Lucas, keeping the departure to himself.

And the suspicion born in the mill began to spawn solid substance in the hunchback's fearful spirit.

'This journey of mine,' he told himself, 'is an amorous strategy elaborated by the magistrate. The declaration I heard him make this afternoon when I was up the vine shows the old fellow from Madrid can't wait any more. No doubt he'll visit the mill tonight, and his first move was to remove me from the scene... But so what? Frasquita is Frasquita, and she won't open up even if they set light to the house!... Even if she did open up, even if the chief magistrate managed to take my excellent Navarrese wife by surprise, the rogue would leave hands on head. Frasquita is Frasquita! Nevertheless,' he added a moment later, 'it would be a good idea to get home as soon as I can tonight!'

With that old Lucas and the constable reached the village and made for the mayor's house.

17

A tin-pot mayor

As an individual and mayor, Juan López was tyranny, brutality and arrogance personified (when dealing with his inferiors), yet he deigned, notwithstanding, at such late hours, after he'd dispatched official business and farm matters and given his wife her daily beating, to drink a pitcher of wine with his secretary and sacristan, an operation that was half complete that night when the miller walked in.

'Hello, old Lucas!' came his greeting, as he scratched his head to tap into his vein of deceit. 'How's your health? Come on, secretary, pour old Lucas a glass of wine! And Señora Frasquita? As beautiful as ever? It's a long time since I saw her! But what a good life you get from your grinding these days! Your rye bread is like manna from heaven! Well... how are you?... Sit down. Take it easy. Thanks be to God, we're in no rush.'

'For my part, damn the grinding!' replied old Lucas, who had kept his lips sealed till then, but whose suspicions grew by the minute when he got such a friendly welcome after that ominous summons.

'Besides, old Lucas,' the mayor continued, 'as you're not in a great rush, you can sleep here tonight, and we'll do our business early in the morning…'

'That's ideal…' old Lucas replied sarcastically, in a deceitful tone quite on a par with Juan López's diplomacy. 'As it's not urgent… I'll spend a night away from home.'

'It's not dangerous or urgent for you,' added the mayor deceived by the man he thought to deceive. 'You can forget all your cares. Hey, Toñuelo… Remove that half-sack so old Lucas can sit down.'

'Pour out the next drink!' piped the miller as he sat down.

'Right there!' the mayor retorted, handing him a full decanter.

'It's in steady hands… Take your measure.'

'Here's to your good health!' replied Juan López, drinking half the wine.

'Here's to yours… Señor Mayor,' replied old Lucas, downing the other half.

'Come on, Manuela!' the rustic mayor then shouted. 'Tell your mistress old Lucas is staying the night. Put a bolster down in the granary.'

'Oh, no… No way! I'll sleep in the barn like a king.

'But we're not short of bolsters…'

'I know! But why upset your family! I've brought my cloak…'

'As you like. Manuela! Tell your mistress not to…'

'All I beg of you,' continued old Lucas, yawning horribly, 'is to let me sleep straight away. I did a lot of grinding last night and have had no shut-eye as yet…'

'Agreed!' the mayor regally replied. 'You can retire whenever you want.'

'I think it's high time we retired too,' said the sacristan, peering at the pitcher of wine to assess the remains. 'It must be ten o'clock, if not a little earlier.'

'A quarter to ten…' pronounced the secretary, after circulating the rest of wine for that night.

'Let's to bed then, gentlemen!' exclaimed the host, downing his share.

'See you in the morning, my good sir,' added the miller, drinking his.

'I hope they light your way… Toñuelo! Take old Lucas to the barn!'

'This way, old Lucas!…' Toñuelo responded, taking the pitcher with him, in case there was a drop left.

'See you in the morning, God willing,' added the sacristan, after he'd drained every glass dry.

And stumbled off cheerfully humming the *De profundis*[9].

'Well, sir,' the mayor remarked to the secretary when they were alone. 'Old Lucas suspected nothing. We can sleep peacefully and… much good may it do His Honour!'

18

Where it will be seen that old Lucas was a light sleeper

Within five minutes a man was dangling out of the window in the mayor's barn – a window overlooking a big yard and some twelve feet above the ground.

In the yard was a shelter over a big manger where six or eight horses of various breeds were tied up, although they all belonged to the weaker sex. Horses, mules and donkeys of the stronger sex were lodged elsewhere.

The man untied a jenny that was already saddled, and led it towards the gate; he slid back the bar, undid the lock, cautiously opened the gate and was back in the middle of the countryside.

He now mounted the jenny, dug his heels in and flew like an arrow towards the city, not along the normal track but across sown fields and gullies.

It was old Lucas, on his way to the mill.

19

Voices clamouring in the wilderness

'Mayors trying to catch a man from Archena!' the Murcian muttered. 'Tomorrow I'll see the bishop as a precautionary measure, and describe everything that happened to me this evening. Such haste and secrecy in summoning me at such an unaccustomed hour; telling me to go by myself; talking to me about serving the King, counterfeit coins, and witches, and goblins, and pouring me two glasses of wine to send me off to sleep!… Nothing could be clearer! Ferret brought these orders on behalf of His Honour, and this is the hour when His Honour will have entered the lists against my wife… I bet I'll find him knocking on the mill door! I bet I'll find him inside already!… I bet!… But what am I saying? Do I doubt my good Navarrese wife? That's an insult to the Almighty! She would never!… My Frasquita would never!… Never!… But what am I saying? Is there such a thing as "never" in this world? Wasn't she a beauty who married a hunchback?'

And as he pondered more, the man with the hump began to cry…

Then he halted his donkey in order to calm himself down; he wiped away his tears; sighed deeply; took out his smoking

50

implements; cut and rolled a black tobacco cigarette; then grasped flint, tinder and steel, and with a few strikes sparked a flame.

That very moment he heard a sound of steps coming towards the path some three hundred yards away.

'How careless of me!' he said, 'If the law's after me, these sparks will have betrayed me!'

He snuffed out the light, dismounted and hid behind his jenny.

But the jenny saw things differently and hee-hawed in pleasure.

'Damn you!' shouted old Lucas, attempting to shut her mouth with his hands.

At the same time another hee-haw resounded from the path, in the manner of a gallant riposte.

'We are done for now!' thought the miller. 'The proverb's really right when it says: "Dealing with animals is the worst of all evils!"'

Rambling thus, he remounted his beast, spurred her on and shot off in the opposite direction from the second hee-haw.

What was most strange was that the person riding the responsive stud must have been equally scared of old Lucas, for he left the path to head off over the sown fields in the other direction.

Meanwhile, the Murcian harped on in this mode:

'What a night! What a world! How my life has changed in the past hour! Constables turned bawd; mayors conspiring against my honour; donkeys hee-hawing when there's no need; and in my breast, a wretched heart that dared doubt the most noble woman God ever created! Oh my God, my God! Hurry me to my house and may I find my Frasquita there!'

Old Lucas continued across scrubland and sown fields,

until finally at eleven at night he reached the front door to the mill without further adventures…

'Damn! The door's open!'

20

Doubt and reality

It was open… yet as he left, he'd heard his wife lock, bolt and bar it!

Consequently, only his wife could have opened up.

How? When? Why? As a result of deception? Because of a legal order? Or deliberately and willingly, by virtue of a previous agreement with His Honour?

What would he soon see? Find out? What awaited him inside his own home? Had Señora Frasquita fled the scene? Been kidnapped? Was she dead? Or in his rival's arms?

'The chief magistrate counted on my not showing up tonight…' he muttered darkly. 'The village mayor had his orders to chain me up rather than let me return… Did Frasquita know this? Was she party to the plot? Or was she the victim of a trap, violence or some other infamy?'

The distressed soul wasted no more time on these cruel reflections than it took him to cross the flagstoned square.

The door to the house was also open. The first room (as in all rural abodes) was the kitchen…

Nobody was in the kitchen.

Yet an enormous fire burned in the fireplace… one he'd put out and which he never lit until well into December!

To cap it all, a lighted candle hung from one of the hooks on the door…

What did it all mean? And how was all that paraphernalia for a wakeful conviviality compatible with the deathly silence reigning over the house?

What had happened to his wife?

Then, and only then, did old Lucas notice the clothes spread over the backs of two or three of the chairs placed around the fireplace...

He stared at the clothes, and let out a loud roar, which stuck in his throat and transformed him into one mute, choking, sobbing mass.

The wretched man thought he was drowning, felt his neck with his hands, while, livid, convulsed, his eyes bulging out of their sockets, he contemplated the array of livery, terrified like a criminal in the death cell presented with his gallows' uniform.

Because what he could see there was the purple cloak, three-cornered hat, frock coat and dove-coloured waistcoat, black-silk breeches, white hose, buckled shoes and even the staff, dress sword and gloves of the execrable chief magistrate... What he could see there were the clothes of his shame, the shroud of his good name, the winding sheet of his good fortune!

The fearful musket still occupied the place where his Navarrese wife had left it two hours before...

Old Lucas leapt upon it like a tiger; tested the barrel with the rod and found it was loaded; looked at the stone and found it was in place.

He then turned to the stairs to the bedroom where he had slept so many years with Señora Frasquita and muttered numbly: 'They must be in there!'

He took one step in that direction; and stopped immediately to survey the scene and ensure nobody was watching him...

'Nobody!' he said silently. 'Only God… and this is His will!'

After confirming his sentence in this manner, he made as if to take another step, when his wandering eyes came to rest on a sheet of paper on the table…

Seeing, falling on it and holding it before his eyes were matters of a second.

That paper was the appointment of Señora Frasquita's nephew, signed by Don Eugenio de Zuñiga y Ponce de León!

'This was the price of the sale!' thought old Lucas, stuffing the paper in his mouth to stifle his cries and stoke his rage. 'I feared she loved her family more than she did me! Oh! We never had children!… That's the reason behind all this!'

The wretched man was about to burst into tears once more.

But then his rage surged again, he grimaced horribly and spluttered, but not now with his voice: 'Upstairs! Upstairs!'

And with one hand began to pull himself up the stairs, while the other carried the musket, and the infamous paper between his teeth.

As if to corroborate his quite reasonable suspicions, when he reached the bedroom door (which was shut) he saw beams of light coming through the cracks in the wood and the keyhole.

'They must be in there!' he repeated.

And stopped for a moment, as if to overcome that fresh cup of bitterness.

Then climbed on up… till he got to the bedroom door.

He could hear no sound inside.

'What if nobody were there!' hope timidly whispered in his ear.

But at that very moment the hapless miller heard coughing inside the bedroom…

The magistrate's asthmatic cough!

No doubt about it! There were no landlines in that shipwreck!

The miller smiled horribly in the deep shadows. How could such lightning not flash in the pitch dark? What was the fire of a tempest compared to what sometimes burns in a man's heart?

Nevertheless, old Lucas (such was his temperament, as we've mentioned already) began to calm down, the moment he heard his enemy's cough...

Reality hurts less than doubt. As he himself had told Señora Frasquita that afternoon, from the minute and hour he lost the only faith which was the lifeblood of his soul, he would start to transform into a new man.

Like the Moor of Venice – to whom we have compared his character already – a single blow of disillusion killed all his love and transfigured the nature of his spirit, making him see the world as an alien planet where he had just landed. The only difference was that old Lucas was by nature less tragic, less austere and more selfish than Desdemona's foolish killer.

Strange to recount, though quite predictable! Doubt, or perhaps hope – which in this case is one and the same – returned to mortify him for a second...

'What if I'd made a mistake!' he thought. 'What if it was Frasquita coughing!...'

Tormented by his misfortune, he'd forgotten he'd seen the magistrate's clothes by the fireside; that he'd found the mill door open; that he'd read the certificate to his infamy...

He crouched down to look through the keyhole, trembling, anxious and uncertain.

His line of vision allowed him only a glimpse of a small triangle of bed, part of the bedhead... But that small triangle allowed him to see one end of a pillow, and on that pillow lay the magistrate's head!

More diabolical laughter convulsed the miller's face.

One could say he was happy again…

'I possess the truth!… Now I need time to think!' he murmured, springing to his feet.

He came downstairs as tentatively as he'd climbed up…

'It's a delicate situation… I need time to reflect. I have plenty of time for everything…' he thought as he went down.

And soon he was sat in the middle of the kitchen, his face hidden in his hands.

He stayed like that for some time, until he was disturbed from his meditation by something which hit his foot…

The musket had slipped from his knee to tell him something…

'No! I said, no!' old Lucas muttered, staring at the weapon. 'That would do me no good! Everyone would pity them… and they'd hang me! He's a magistrate… and magistrate-killing still carries the death penalty in Spain! They'd also say I killed him driven by groundless jealousy, and then that I stripped him and put him in my bed… They'd also say I killed my wife out of mere suspicion… They'd hang me! You bet they'd hang me! Besides, I'd have shown I had very little feeling, very little talent, if at the end of my life I were a mere object of pity! I'd be a laughing stock! They'd all say my misfortune was quite natural, given my hunchback and Frasquita's beauty! No, no! I must have revenge, and after my revenge, I must be successful, scornful and laugh – laugh at myself, laugh at everyone, ensure nobody can mock this hump I've almost made an object of envy, and which would look grotesque on the gallows.'

And Lucas' thoughts rambled on – perhaps he wasn't even aware of them; as a result of such thinking, he restored the weapon to its rightful place, and stalked up and down, arms behind back, head lowered, as if searching for revenge on the floor, on the ground, in the pettiness of life, in some shameful, ridiculous practical joke he could play on his wife and the magistrate, far from seeking a similar revenge in law, in a duel, in forgiveness, in heaven... as any other man might have done with a character less opposed to the impositions of Nature, of society or of his own feelings.

Suddenly, his eyes came to rest on the magistrate's apparel...

Then he halted in his tracks...

An expression of indefinable happiness, joy, success spread over his face... till in the end he started to guffaw... huge belly laughs that were silent – so they wouldn't hear him upstairs – he clasped his fists to his sides so they didn't burst, shook like an epileptic, and finally collapsed in a chair till that mood of convulsed, sarcastic bliss passed. It was the laughter of a Mephistopheles.[10]

As soon as he'd recovered his calm, he feverishly stripped off his clothes; placed them all on the same chairs where he'd found the magistrate's; donned all the garments that belonged to the latter, from buckled shoes to three-cornered hat; girt his dress sword; wrapped round his purple cloak; picked up his staff and gloves, left the mill and headed for the city, swaying like Don Eugenio de Zuñiga, and occasionally muttering this sentence, which mirrored his thoughts:

'The magistrate's wife is beautiful too!'

21

En garde, *good sir*

Let's leave old Lucas for now, and find out what happened at the mill from the time we left Señora Frasquita alone there till her husband returned to discover an earth-shaking change…

An hour must have passed after old Lucas' departure in the company of Toñuelo before the downcast Navarran decided not to go to bed till her husband returned; she was knitting in her bedroom on the top floor, when she heard pitiful cries from outside the house, from very close by, from the mill race.

'Help, I'm drowning! Frasquita! Frasquita!…' a man's voice shouted out dismally, desperately.

'Perhaps it's Lucas?' thought the Navarran woman, filled with a terror we have no need to describe.

The same bedroom had a small door, which Ferret has already informed us about, and which in effect looked down over the highest part of the mill race. Señora Frasquita opened it unhesitatingly, though she hadn't recognised the voice clamouring for help and found herself face to face with the chief magistrate climbing dripping wet out of the stream…

'God forgive me! God forgive me!' stammered the infamous old man. 'I thought I was drowning!'

'What! You! What do you mean by this? How dare you? Why are you back at this time of night?' shouted the miller's wife, indignant rather than afraid, retreating instinctively.

'Be quiet, woman!' lisped His Honour, slipping into the room after her. 'I'll tell you everything… I almost drowned! The water swept me along like a leaf. Look at the state I'm in!'

'Out! Get out of here!' Señora Frasquita rasped even

more violently. 'I don't need your explanations!… I can see everything only too clearly! What do I care if you drown? Did I invite you here? Oh! What shame! That's why you put the summons out on my husband!'

'Listen, woman…'

'I won't listen! Clear off, Your Honour, right now!… Clear off or I won't be responsible for your life!'

'What do you mean?'

'You heard! My husband isn't at home, but I'm strong enough to defend his self-respect! Clear off the way you came, or these hands of mine will throw you back into the water!'

'My dear girl! Don't create so, I'm not deaf!' exclaimed the old libertine. 'If I'm here, it's for a good reason! I've come to liberate old Lucas, who's been taken prisoner mistakenly by the local mayor… But, first, you must dry my clothes… I'm soaked to the skin!'

'I told you to clear off!'

'Shut up, you fool!… Don't you know who I am?… Look… here's your nephew's appointment… Light the fire, and let's talk… While my clothes dry, I'll get into this bed.'

'Ah! So you admit you were after me? So you admit that's why you had my Lucas arrested? So you've brought the appointment with you? By all the saints in heaven! Who does this joker think I am?'

'Frasquita! I am the chief magistrate!'

'You could be the king, for all I care! I am my husband's wife, and mistress of my house! Do you think I'm scared of magistrates? I will go to Madrid, and to the ends of the earth, to seek justice against a dirty old man who drags his authority through the mud like you! What's more, tomorrow I'll put on my mantilla and go to see Her Ladyship…'

'You, my dear, will do nothing of the kind!' the magistrate

riposted, losing patience and changing tactics. 'You'll do nothing of the kind; because I'll shoot you if you won't accept my reasoning…'

'Shoot me!' exclaimed Señora Frasquita, rather subdued.

'Shoot you, that's right… and I won't suffer one jot. I happen to have told people in the city that I was going to spend the night hunting brigands… So, deary, don't be silly… love me… like I adore you!'

'Shoot me, Your Honour?' repeated the Navarran, flinging her arms behind her and thrusting her body forwards as if to leap on her adversary.

'If you carry on like this, I'll snuff you out and be spared your beauty and your threats…' His Honour timorously replied, taking out a pair of pistols.

'So pistols in one pocket? And my nephew's appointment in the other!' said Señora Frasquita, her head bobbing up and down. 'Well, sir, that's not a difficult choice. Good sir, just wait a moment, while I light the fire.'

And with these words she walked quickly to the stairs and reached the bottom in three leaps.

His Honour took the light, and pursued the miller's wife, afraid she would escape; but he had to descend much more slowly, so by the time he reached the kitchen, he bumped into Señora Frasquita on her way back after him.

'So you reckoned you were going to take a shot at me?' enquired that formidable lady, taking a step backwards. 'Well, *en garde*, good sir; I'm ready for you!'

Saying this, she lifted up the awesome musket that plays such an important part in this story.

'Wait, you wretched woman! What do you think you're doing?' shouted the magistrate, scared stiff. 'I was only joking about taking a shot… Look… my pistols aren't even loaded.

On the other hand, the appointment's for real... Here you are... Take it... It's a present. No strings attached...'

And he shook as he put it on the table.

'Leave it right there!' retorted the Navarran. 'It will do to light the fire with tomorrow, when I get my husband's lunch. I don't want the stench of your power and glory; and, if my nephew were to come from Estella at some stage, he'd stamp on the ugly hand which inscribed his name on that obscene paper! Go on! I told you! Clear out of my house! Out, out, out!... Quick... the powder's rising to my head!'

The chief magistrate didn't reply. He had turned livid, if not blue; his eyes bulged, a dengue-style fever shook his whole body. Finally, his teeth started to chatter, and he hit the ground, felled by an awesome convulsion.

His fear of the mill race, his sopping-wet clothes, the violent bedroom scene and his horror at the musket the Navarran aimed at him had exhausted any strength the sickly old man had. 'I'm dying!' he stammered. 'Call Ferret!... Call Ferret who must be out there... on the path... I can't die in this house!...'

He could say no more. He shut his eyes and acted as if dead.

'And he'll die as he says he will!' Señora Frasquita shouted. 'This is my darkest hour! What can I do with this man in my house? What will people say about me if he were to die? What would Lucas say? How could I defend myself, when I myself opened the door to him? No... I can't stay here. I must find my husband. I'll shock society rather than tarnish my honour!'

After she'd come to this decision, she dropped the musket, went into the yard, took the donkey that was still there, quickly saddled it, opened the main gate in the big fence, mounted her steed with one jump, notwithstanding her weight, and headed for the dirt track.

'Ferret! Ferret!' shouted the woman from Navarre, as she closed in on his hiding place.

'Here I am!' the constable replied, popping up from behind a hedge. 'Is that you, Señora Frasquita?'

'Yes, it's me. Go to the mill, to your master, who's dying and who needs help…'

'What's that?'

'You heard me, Ferret…'

'And where are you headed at this time of night?'

'Me… I'm off to the city for a doctor!' answered Señora Frasquita, digging a heel into her donkey and a foot into Ferret's backside.

And she took… not the path to the city, as she'd said, but to the neighbouring village.

Ferret didn't notice this detail, for he was hurtling towards the mill, mumbling to himself:

'She's gone to fetch a doctor… It's the least the wretched woman can do. But what a clueless fellow! A fine time to fall sick!… God gives sugared almonds to men who can't nibble!'

22

Ferret everywhere

When Ferret reached the mill, the magistrate was beginning to come round and trying to pick himself up from the floor.

On the floor, by his side, was the lighted candle he'd brought down from the bedroom.

'She gone yet?' were Don Eugenio's first words.

'Who?'

'The she-devil!… I mean the miller's wife.'

'Yes, sir… She's gone… and not in the best of tempers…'

'Oh, Ferret! I'm dying…'

'But what's wrong, Excellency? For heaven's sake!'

'I fell in the mill race, and I'm soaked… chilled to the marrow!'

'Well, well! We are in a fine mess!'

'Ferret!… Watch what you say!'

'I didn't say a word, sir…'

'Well, then, get me out of this scrape…'

'I'm on the job right away… Your Excellency will see how I soon sort everything out!'

After he'd said that, in a jiffy the constable picked up the light with one hand and put His Honour under his arm with the other and pulled him up to the bedroom; stripped him; put him in bed; ran to the winepress; gathered a bundle of wood; went to the kitchen; made a big fire; placed all his master's clothes downstairs on the backs of two or three chairs; lit a candle; hung it on the back of the door and clambered back up to the bedroom.

'How're we doing?' he asked Don Eugenio, lifting up his oil lamp to get a better view of his face.

'Wonderfully well! I'm going to sweat some! And tomorrow I'm going to hang you, Ferret!'

'Why, sir?'

'You've the cheek to ask me? When you laid your plans for me, do you think I was expecting to find myself alone in this bed, after receiving the sacrament of baptism for a second time? I'll hang you bright and early!'

'But tell me something, Your Excellency?… Señora Frasquita?…'

'Señora Frasquita tried to murder me. That's all I got from

following your advice! I'll hang you at the crack of dawn.'

'It can't be as bad as that, Your Honour!' retorted the constable.

'And how do you work that out, you insolent so-and-so? Because I'm flat on my back?'

'No, sir. I say so because Señora Frasquita can't have been as cruel as Your Honour describes for she's gone to get you a doctor from the city…'

'Holy God! Are you sure she's gone to the city?' shouted Don Eugenio, beside himself more than ever.

'At least, that's what she told me…'

'Run, Ferret, run! Oh! I am done for now! Do you know why Señora Frasquita has gone to the city? To tell my wife everything!… To tell her I'm here! Oh my God! Could I ever have imagined this? I thought she'd go to the village after her husband; and as I've got him well cared for there, I wasn't worried about her leaving! But if she goes to the city!… Run, Ferret, run… You're light-footed. Make sure I'm not ruined! Stop the awful miller's wife from entering my house!'

'And Your Honour won't hang me if I'm successful?' rejoined the constable ironically.

'On the contrary! I'll give you a really fine pair of shoes that are too big for me. I'll give you whatever you ask for!'

'I'm off then. Sleep sweetly. I'll be back in half an hour after clapping that Navarran woman in jail. It's not for nothing I'm quicker than an ass!'

Ferret spoke, then disappeared downstairs.

Needless to say, it was during the constable's absence that the miller returned to the mill and had his visions through the keyhole.

For our part, we'll leave His Honour to sweat in someone else's bed, and Ferret to rush to the city (where shortly old

Lucas followed him in three-cornered hat and purple cloak), and, transforming ourselves into cross-country runners, we too would fly to the village in pursuit of the valiant Señora Frasquita.

23

Back to the wilderness and voices you might expect

The only adventure the Navarran had on her journey from mill to village was to take fright when she noticed someone making sparks in the middle of a field.

'Perhaps it's one of His Honour's flunkeys? What if he arrests me?' thought the miller's wife.

And she heard a hee-haw from the same direction.

'Donkeys abroad at this late hour!' thought Señora Frasquita. 'There is no farm or homestead around here… I swear to God the little folk are having a ball tonight!'

The donkey Señora Frasquita was riding also thought it a good time to hee-haw.

'Be quiet, you pest!' the Navarran told him, sticking a long pin into his withers.

And, afraid of an inopportune encounter, she also rode her steed off the path and trotted through other fields.

Without further misadventure, she reached the gates to the village at about an hour before midnight.

24

A king for the times

His master the mayor was sleeping deeply, back to back with his wife (thus creating the *double-headed eagle* of the Austrias, as our immortal Quevedo has it), when Toñuelo knocked on the door to the nuptial chamber. And informed Juan López that Señora Frasquita, the woman from the mill, wanted to talk to him.

No reason to describe all the grunts and oaths inherent in the tin-pot mayor's act of waking up and dressing, so we'll quickly shift to the moment the miller's wife saw him loom up, stretching like a gymnast exercising his muscles, and exclaiming with an endless yawn:

'A hearty welcome to you, Señora Frasquita! What brings you to these parts? Didn't Toñuelo tell you to stay at the mill? Do you always disobey the authorities thus?'

'I must see my Lucas!' replied the Navarran. 'I must see him at once! Tell him his wife is here!'

' "I must! I must!" Señora, you forget you are speaking to the King!…'

'Forget the King nonsense, Señor Juan, for I'm in no joking mood! You know only too well what I've been going through! And only too well why you've locked up my husband!'

'I know nothing, Señora Frasquita… And as for your husband, he's not locked up but sleeping peacefully in this his house, treated the way I treat people. Come on, Toñuelo! Toñuelo! Get along to the barn and tell old Lucas to wake up and present himself here sharpish… So you were… Tell me what's up!… Were you afraid to sleep alone?'

'Don't be so thick-skinned, Señor Juan! You know I hate

your jokes and jibes! What I've been going through is very simple: you and His Honour tried to ruin me! But I've really disappointed you! I come here unblushing, and His Honour is back at the mill dying!...'

'The chief magistrate dying!' shouted his subordinate. 'Señora, do you realise what you are saying?'

'You heard me! He fell into the mill race, and almost drowned, or caught pneumonia, or whatever... That's down to Her Ladyship! I've come for my husband, and intend to go to Madrid tomorrow...'

'Damn, damn, damn!' muttered Juan López. 'Hey, Manuela!... Hey, wench!...'

'Go saddle my mule... Señora Frasquita, I'll go to the mill... Woe betide you if you hurt His Honour in any way!'

'Señor Mayor, Señor Mayor!' exclaimed Toñuelo at that instant, walking in more dead than alive. 'Old Lucas isn't in the barn. His jenny isn't in the stables, and the yard gate is open... The bird has flown!'

'What are you saying?' shouted Señor Juan López.

'By the Virgen del Carmen! What will happen at home?' Señora Frasquita exclaimed. 'Let's make haste, Señor Mayor: and waste no time!... My husband will kill the magistrate if he finds him there at this time of day...'

'Then you think old Lucas has gone to the mill?'

'Of course! What's more, I crossed his path on my way here but didn't realise... He must have been the one making sparks fly in the middle of a field! My God! When one thinks how animals understand more than humans! Because I can tell you, Señor Juan, that for sure our two donkeys recognised and greeted each other, whereas my Lucas and I didn't greet or recognise one another... Rather we fled in opposite directions, thinking we were spies!...'

'A fine fellow that Lucas of yours!' replied the mayor. 'Anyway, let's get on, and then we'll decide what we'll do with the pair of you. Don't fool around with me! I am the King!... But not a king like the one we've now got in El Pardo; I'm like the one there was in Seville once, the one they called Don Pedro the Cruel. Come on, Manuela! Bring me my stick, and tell your mistress I'm leaving!'

The servant (who was certainly a wench too pretty for the moral mayoress) obeyed and, as Juan López's mule was already saddled up, Señora Frasquita and he left for the mill, followed by the indispensable Toñuelo.

25

A ferret's star

Let's ride on ahead of them, since we have carte blanche to move on faster than anyone.

Ferret was already back at the mill, after hunting for Señora Frasquita down every street in the city.

The cunning constable had stopped by the magistrate's house, where he'd found everything very quiet. The doors were still open as at midday, as is the usual custom when the powers-that-be are out in the street, exercising their hallowed functions. Other constables and officials were dozing in the stairwell and porch, waiting for their master to return; when they heard Ferret arrive, two or three stretched out their limbs and asked their immediate boss:

'Is the master on his way?'

'Not likely! Be quiet. I've come to see if anything untoward has happened here...'

'Nothing we noticed.'

'And Her Ladyship?'

'Resting in her chambers.'

'No woman walked through these doors a minute ago?'

'Nobody's showed up all night!…'

'Well, don't let anyone in, whoever it is and whatever they say. On the contrary! Grab any early-morning bird who comes asking after His Honour or Ladyship, and clap them in jail!'

'So tonight the hunt's on for serious game?' enquired one of the beadles.

'Big game!' another added.

'Right royal!' responded Ferret solemnly. 'Imagine how tricky things must be if His Honour and me are doing our own beating!… So, be good and keep a watchful eye out!'

'May God go with you, Señor Bastián,' they all bid Ferret farewell.

'My star is on the wane!' mumbled the latter as he left the magistrate's house. 'Even women are conning me! The miller's went to the village after her husband, rather than coming to the city… Wretched Ferret! Whatever became of your nose?'

And, muttering thus, he followed the path to the mill.

The constable was right to lament his loss of nose, for he didn't scent a man right there hiding behind the willows, quite near the path, who shouted into his cape or rather his purple cloak:

'Take care, Pablo! Ferret's coming this way!… He mustn't see me…'

It was old Lucas dressed up as the magistrate, heading towards the city, repeating from time to time his diabolical sentence:

'The magistrate's wife is also beautiful!'

Ferret went by without noticing him, and the fake magistrate left his hiding place and penetrated the city streets...

A moment later the constable reached the mill, as we've already mentioned.

26

Reaction

The magistrate was still in bed, exactly as old Lucas had just seen him through the keyhole.

'I'm in a real sweat, Ferret! I saved myself from sickness!' he exclaimed as the constable entered the room. 'And Señora Frasquita? Did you get her? Have you brought her with you? Did she speak to Her Ladyship?'

'The miller's wife, sir,' responded Ferret in anguished tones, 'deceived me like a simpleton; for she didn't go to the city, but to the village... after her husband.'

'It gets better and better!' retorted the man from Madrid, his eyes glinting evilly. 'All is saved! Before dawn breaks, Señora Frasquita and old Lucas will be on the road to the prisons of the Inquisition, tied elbow to elbow, and they'll rot there with nobody to tell of their adventures this night. Bring me my clothes, Ferret, for they must be dry by now... Bring them and dress me! The lover is going to change back into the magistrate!...'

Ferret went downstairs to fetch his clothes from the kitchen.

27

In the name of the King!

Meanwhile, Señora Frasquita, Señor Juan López and Toñuelo advanced to the mill, where they were shortly to arrive.

'I will enter first!' exclaimed the tin-pot mayor. 'That's why I am in authority! Follow me, Toñuelo, and you, Señora Frasquita, wait by the door till I summon you.'

So Señor Juan López walked under the vine, where, in the moonlight, he saw an almost hunchbacked man, dressed like the miller, with a waistcoat and grey cloth breeches, a black sash, blue stockings, a felt Murcian hat, and a riding cape over his shoulder.

'There he is!' shouted the mayor. 'In the name of the King! Give yourself up, old Lucas!'

The man in the hat tried to run inside the mill.

'Got you!' shouted Toñuelo, jumping on him, grabbing him by the scruff of his neck, digging a knee into his spine and putting him to the ground. At the same time, another species of animal jumped on Toñuelo, and grabbed him by the waist, knocked him on the flagstones, and started hitting.

It was Señora Frasquita, who was shouting:

'Rascal! Let go of my Lucas!'

But, at that moment, another person, who had appeared leading a donkey by his right hand, intervened resolutely between the two of them, and tried to rescue Toñuelo…

It was Ferret, who had mistaken the local constable for Don Eugenio de Zuñiga and was shouting at the miller's wife:

'Señora, have some respect for my master!'

And he knocked her on top of the villager.

Señora Frasquita, seeing herself caught in the crossfire,

then came down heavily on the middle of Ferret's stomach, and made him fall flat on his face.

And so there were four people rolling around on the ground.

Señor Juan López, meanwhile, prevented the so-called old Lucas from getting up by planting a foot on his back.

'Ferret! Help! In the name of the King! I am the chief magistrate!' Don Eugenio finally shouted, feeling that the mayor's hoof, shod in bull's leather, was materially destroying him.

'The magistrate! Oh, so it is!' said a surprised Juan López.

'The magistrate!' they all repeated. And soon the four who'd been floored were back on their feet.

'To jail with the lot of you!' cried Don Eugenio de Zuñiga. 'To the gallows, the lot of you!'

'But, sir...' interrupted Juan López, kneeling down. 'Forgive the mistreatment! But how could we recognise you in these clothes?'

'Fool!' retorted the magistrate. 'I had to wear something! Don't you realise mine were stolen? Don't you realise a band of thieves headed by old Lucas?...'

'Liar!' shouted the Navarrese woman.

'Listen to me, Señora Frasquita,' said Ferret pulling her to one side. 'With the permission of the magistrate and company... If you don't sort this out, they'll hang the lot of us, starting with old Lucas!...'

'Why? What's happened?' asked Señora Frasquita.

'Only that old Lucas is prowling round the city dressed as the magistrate... God knows whether his disguise has got him into His Ladyship's bedroom.'

And the constable recounted in four words all that we already know.

'Jesus!' exclaimed the miller's wife. 'So my husband thinks I'm dishonoured! And he's gone to the city to take his revenge! We must go to the city, and I must clear myself in the eyes of my Lucas!'

'We must go to the city and stop that man from talking to my wife and telling her all that nonsense he's imagined!' said the magistrate, mounting one of the donkeys.

'Give me a help up with your foot, mayor.'

'Yes, we must go to the city...' added Ferret, 'and, chief magistrate, let's hope to high heaven that old Lucas, aided by your garb, has done no more than talk to Her Ladyship!'

'What do you mean, wretch?' Don Eugenio de Zuñiga interrupted. 'Do you think that peasant capable?...'

'Of anything!' answered Señora Frasquita.

28

Ave Maria Purisima!
Half-past twelve and all is quiet!

That was the cry sung on the streets of the city by the night watchman when the miller's wife and the magistrate, each riding one of the mill donkeys, Señor Juan López on his mule, and the two constables on foot, reached the door to the magistrate's house.

The door was shut.

One could say all business had been concluded for the day for both government and governed.

'Looks bad!' thought Ferret.

And rapped the knocker two or three times.

A long time passed before anyone opened or answered.

Señora Frasquita was more yellow than beeswax.

The magistrate had already chewed all his fingernails.

Bang!… Bang!… Bang!… More loud knocks on the door to the magistrate's house (applied successively by the two constables and by Señor Juan López)… Nothing doing. Nobody replied! Nobody opened up! Not a squeak! The only sound to be heard was from the spouts of a fountain in the house's courtyard.

And eternally long minutes ensued.

Finally, at about one o'clock, a small second-floor window opened and a female voice said:

'Who goes there?'

'It's the wet nurse…' Ferret mumbled.

'It is I!' thundered Don Eugenio de Zuñiga. 'Open up!'

A minute's silence followed.

'And who might you be?' retorted the wet nurse.

'Can't you hear who I am? I am the master!… The magistrate!…'

Another pause followed.

'May God go with you!' the good woman replied. 'My master came here an hour ago and took to his bed straight away. You can all go to bed now and sleep off your skinfuls!'

And the window slammed shut.

Señora Frasquita covered her face with her hands.

'You, wet nurse!' thundered the magistrate, beside himself. 'Don't you hear me ordering you to open the door? Can't you hear who I am? Do you want me to hang you as well?'

The window flew open again.

'What's all this? Who are you to shout so?'

'I am the chief magistrate!'

'Still singing the same tune! Didn't I tell you that the magistrate came in before midnight… and with my very own eyes I saw him close the doors to Her Ladyship's chambers? Are you playing games with me? Just you wait and see what happens!'

The door suddenly opened and a crowd of servants and minions, armed with clubs, threw itself upon those outside, shouting furiously:

'Come on then! Where's the fellow who says he's the chief magistrate? Where's that scoundrel? Where's that drunk?'

And there was one hell of a mêlée in the pitch dark and nobody could hear anyone. And the magistrate, Ferret, Señor Juan López and Toñuelo all got a good hiding.

It was the second thrashing that night's excursion had cost Don Eugenio, not to mention the drenching in the mill race.

Señora Frasquita, on the edge of that abyss, cried for the first time in her life…

'Lucas! Lucas!' she was saying. 'You doubted me! Your arms embraced another woman! Ay! Our shame cannot be undone!'

29

Post-nuptial… Diana

'What is this to-do?' a calm, majestic, gracious voice finally asked, resounding above the mayhem.

They all looked up and saw a woman in black, peering over the main balcony.

'Our Ladyship!' chorused the servants, interrupting the round of blows.

'My wife!' stammered Don Eugenio.

'Let these countryfolk in… The magistrate says to allow

this…' the magistrate's wife added.

The servants stood aside, and de Zuñiga and companions went in the front door and headed upstairs.

No criminal has climbed the gallows as insecure and pallid as the magistrate climbed the stairs in his own house. Nevertheless, the idea of his own dishonour was beginning to predominate – ever nobly selfish – over all the misfortunes which he had caused and which afflicted him, and over the other many absurdities of the situation in which he found himself…

'Most of all,' he was thinking, 'I am a Zuñiga y Ponce de León!… Woe betide anyone who forgets that! Woe betide my wife if she has disgraced my name!'

30

A lady of class

Her Ladyship received her husband and his rustic cortège in the main room of the magistrate's house.

She stood alone, her eyes staring at the door.

She was a most distinguished lady, still fairly young, a beauty at once serene and severe, more suited to a Christian than a pagan brush, and was dressed as nobly and seriously as the tastes of the time allowed. Her black dress, with its short, narrow skirt and loose, high sleeves, was of Aleppo wool; a white lace shawl with a yellowish tint veiled her wondrous shoulders, and long, black tulle draped most of her alabaster arms. She cooled herself majestically with an enormous fan from the Philippines, while her other hand held a lace handkerchief, the four corners of which hung down in a symmetrical neatness only comparable to her own attitude and slightest movement.

That beautiful woman was rather regal, with more than a touch of the prioress, and hence she inspired veneration and fear in all who looked upon her. Besides, the elegance of her dress at that late hour and the brilliant lights which lit the room, showed the magistrate's wife had taken the utmost care to lend the scene a theatrical, ceremonial solemnity in contrast to the cheap, obscene character of her husband's adventure.

Finally, we should note that that lady went by the name of Doña Mercedes Carrillo de Albornoz y Espinosa de los Monteros, and she was daughter, granddaughter, great- grand-daughter, great-great-granddaughter and granddaughter to the *n*th degree of the city, as well as a descendant of its most illustrious conquerors. For reasons of mundane vanity, her family had persuaded her to marry the old, wealthy magistrate, for otherwise she would have become a nun, since her natural vocation inclined her towards the cloister, to the acceptance of that painful sacrifice.

At the same time she already had two offspring from that boorish man from Madrid, and there were even rumours of other innocents abroad…

And so to resume our thread…

3 1

The law of a tooth for a tooth

'Mercedes!' the magistrate clamoured as he entered the presence of his wife.

'Hello, old Lucas! What can we do for you?' the

magistrate's wife interjected. 'Has there been a disaster at the mill?'

'My Ladyship, I am in no joking mood!' retorted the magistrate in a rage. 'Before I embark on any explanations, I demand to know what has become of my honour…'

'That does not depend on me! Did you perchance put it into safekeeping with me?'

'Yes, my lady… with you!' responded Don Eugenio. 'Wives safekeep their husband's honour!'

'Well, then, dear old Lucas, better ask your wife… She's right there listening to us.'

Señora Frasquita, who had stayed by the door, bellowed curiously.

'Come in, madam, and sit down…' the magistrate's wife added, addressing the miller's wife in regal, dignified tones.

And, for her own part, she walked towards the sofa.

The generous Navarrese woman immediately understood the grandeur in the attitude of that affronted… perhaps doubly affronted wife… So, immediately rising to similar peaks, she reined in her natural impetuosity and kept a decorous silence. Naturally, there's no need to add that Señora Frasquita, confident of her innocence and strength, didn't rush to defend herself, though she had plenty of reason to level accusations… though certainly not at Her Ladyship. She wanted to settle accounts with old Lucas… and old Lucas was nowhere to be seen!

'Señora Frasquita…' the noble lady repeated, seeing the miller's wife had not budged from where she was, 'I asked you to come in and sit down.'

Her second address was more affectionate than the first… One might say that the magistrate's wife had also instinctively guessed, on perceiving that woman's calm demeanour and manly beauty, that she was not dealing with a lowly, contemptible being but rather with someone as unfortunate as herself; unfortunate, that is, if only because she'd become acquainted with the magistrate!

Those two women who once considered themselves to be rivals now exchanged looks of peace and compassion, and noted to their great surprise that their souls reached out to each other, like two sisters recognising themselves as such.

Just as the chaste snows of lofty mountain peaks perceive and greet one another.

Savouring these sweet emotions, the miller's wife swept majestically into the room, and sat down on the edge of a chair.

When she passed through the mill, foreseeing she might be making visitations of some importance, she had smartened herself up and put on a large, tasselled, black flannel mantilla that fitted her divinely. She seemed a real lady.

As far as the magistrate is concerned, no need to say he had kept silent during that scene. Señora Frasquita's roar and appearance on the scene had startled him. The woman terrified him more than his wife!

'So, then, old Lucas…' Doña Mercedes proceeded to address her husband. 'Here is Señora Frasquita… Pray pose your questions a second time! Quiz her about that honour of yours!'

'Mercedes, by the sores of our Saviour!' the magistrate shouted. 'You obviously don't know what I'm capable of! I beseech you yet again to stop playing games and tell me everything that has happened during my absence! Where is that fellow?'

'Who? My husband?… My husband's getting up and will be here in no time.'

'Getting up!' bawled Don Eugenio.

79

'Does that surprise you? Well, where would you expect an honourable man to be at this hour of the night if not at home, and at home sleeping with his legitimate consort, as God bids?'

'Merceditas! Careful what you say! Remember who's listening! Remember I am the chief magistrate!…'

'Don't you start shouting at me, old Lucas, or I'll tell these constables to lock you up!' responded the magistrate's wife, getting to her feet.

'Lock me up! Me! The city's chief magistrate!'

'The city's chief magistrate, representative of law and order, appointee of the King,' the great lady replied severely, forcefully, drowning out the fake miller's voice, 'reached home at the proper time, to rest from the noble tasks of office, in order the morrow to continue protecting its citizens' honour and lives, the sanctity of the hearth, and respect of its women, thus to prevent anyone from entering the bedroom of anybody else's wife, disguised as a magistrate or anything else; to prevent anyone from offending virtue in its proper repose or disturbing its chaste slumbers…'

'Merceditas! What are you suggesting?' whistled the magistrate between lip and gum. 'If it's true that has happened in my house, I say you are a perfidious, licentious wench!'

'Who does this man think he is talking to?' the magistrate's wife interrupted him scornfully, casting her eyes over all those present. 'Who is this lunatic? This drunkard?… I can no longer believe he is an honest miller like old Lucas, though he's wearing his rustic clothes! Señor Juan López, believe me,' she continued, addressing the terrified village mayor, 'My husband, the magistrate of this city, reached his house two hours ago, wearing his three-cornered hat, purple cloak and dress sword and wielding his staff of office… The servants and constables now listening to me got up to greet him when they saw him walk through the door, up the stairs and into the reception. Immediately, all doors were locked and after that nobody entered my home until you arrived. Isn't this true? You tell them.'

'It's true! It's true!' the wet nurse, servants and minions cried; all those grouped around the door to that room to witness such a singular scene.

'Everybody out of here!' shouted Don Eugenio, foaming with rage. 'Ferret! Ferret! Come and arrest these vile wretches who show no respect to me! Jail the lot! Hang the lot!'

Ferret was nowhere to be seen.

'Moreover, sir…' continued Doña Mercedes, changing tone and now condescending to look at her husband and to treat him as such, fearful these pranks might reach irrevocable extremes, 'just suppose you are my husband… Just suppose you are Don Eugenio de Zuñiga y Ponce de León.'

'I am!'

'Moreover, just suppose I was at all at fault when I mistook for you the man who entered my bedroom dressed as a magistrate…'

'Foul scum!' the old man screamed, reaching for his sword, and finding only an empty space, or the Murcian miller's sash.

The Navarran covered her face with one side of her mantilla to hide her flaming jealousy.

'Just suppose whatever you want,' continued Doña Mercedes, inexplicably impassive. 'Pray tell me now, my sir, would you have any right to complain? Could you accuse me as my prosecutor? Could you sentence me as my judge? Have you just come from the confessional? Have you just heard Mass? Why do you come here in such garb? Why do you come here with that lady? Where have you spent half the night?'

'Let me…' interrupted Señora Frasquita, rising to her feet as if impelled by a spring and pushing herself arrogantly between wife and husband.

The latter, who was about to speak, stood and gaped as the Navarrese woman entered the lists.

But Doña Mercedes anticipated her, and said:

'Madame, don't wear yourself out giving me explanations. I don't expect any at all from you… Here comes the man who may rightly ask for them… Make your peace with him!'

Simultaneously a side door opened and old Lucas walked in, dressed from head to foot like a magistrate, and with staff, gloves and dress sword as if he were making an appearance in the council chambers.

32

Faith moves mountains

'And a very good night to you all,' the newcomer declared, removing his three-cornered hat, and talking out of his sunken mouth, like Don Eugenio de Zuñiga.

He advanced across the room, swaying in every sense of the word, and went to kiss the hand of the magistrate's wife.

Everyone was taken aback. So striking was old Lucas' similarity with the real magistrate.

So much so that the servants, and even Señor Juan López, couldn't stifle their guffaws.

Don Eugenio felt that fresh insult, and pounced upon old Lucas like a dragon.

But Señora Frasquita intervened, the aforesaid arm repelling the magistrate.

Old Lucas turned paler than death when he saw his wife walk towards him; but then he restrained himself, and with a horrible cackle that made you put your hand to your heart to stop it bursting, he said, still imitating the magistrate:

'God keep you, Frasquita! Have you sent your nephew his appointment?'

You should have seen the Navarran then! She flung off her mantilla, lifted her forehead like a regal lioness, and transfixed the fake magistrate with eyes like daggers.

'I've nothing but contempt for you, Lucas!' she told him to his face.

Everybody thought she'd spat on him.

Such were the gesture, grimace and tone of voice which underlined that sentence!

The miller's face transfigured when he heard his wife's voice. Inspiration like religious faith had penetrated his soul, suffused it with light and happiness... And so, for a moment he forgot all he had seen or thought he'd seen in the mill, and exclaimed with tears in his eyes and sincerity on his lips:

'So you are my Frasquita?'

'No!' responded the Navarran beside herself. 'I am no longer your Frasquita! I am... Ask your evening's exploits and they'll tell you what you've done to the heart which loved you so much!...'

And she burst into tears, like a mountain of ice beginning to melt and break up.

The magistrate's wife moved spontaneously towards her and embraced her most tenderly.

Then Señora Frasquita started to kiss her, not knowing what she was doing either, muttering as she sobbed, like a child seeking a mother's solace:

'Señora, señora! I am so unhappy!'

'Not so much as you think you are!' replied the magistrate's wife, also crying copiously.

'I really am unhappy,' moaned old Lucas at the same time, fighting down his tears, as if ashamed to shed them.

'And what about me?' Don Eugenio finally enquired, mellowed by the contagious weeping of the others, or perhaps hoping to be saved from the path of moisture, or, rather, the path of the lamentation. 'As for me! I'm a villain! A monster! A no-good miscreant who's got his just desserts!'

And he began to whimper pathetically as he embraced Señor Juan López's belly.

And the latter and the servants also cried, and it all seemed at an end, and yet nobody had explained him or herself.

33

And how was it for you?

Old Lucas was the first to swim to the surface of that sea of tears.

The fact was he started to recall what he'd seen through the keyhole.

'Gentlemen, let's get down to brass tacks!…' he bellowed suddenly.

'This is no brass-tack matter, old Lucas,' responded the magistrate's wife. 'That wife of yours is a real saint!'

'Well… yes… but…'

'No buts about it!… Let her say her piece, and you'll see how she defends herself. As soon as I saw her, my heart told me she was a saint in spite of everything you'd told me.'

'All right, let her speak!' old Lucas urged.

'I've nothing to say!' answered the miller's wife. 'You're the one with the explaining to do… Because the truth is you…'

And Señora Frasquita said no more because of the prodigious respect the magistrate's wife inspired in her.

'Well, what about you?' retorted old Lucas, losing faith once more.

'It's got nothing to do with her…' the magistrate shouted, feeling his jealousy rise. 'It's to do with you and this lady! Oh, Merceditas!… Who could ever have told me that you?…'

'And what about you?' retorted his wife, looking him straight in the eye.

And for a few moments the two couples repeated the same phrases:

'And you?'

'Well, what about you?'

'How was it for you?'

'No, you?'

'But, how could you?…'

Etcetera, etcetera, etcetera.

It would have gone on for ever if the magistrate's wife, regaining her dignity, hadn't finally said to Don Eugenio:

'Shut up! We'll settle our private business later. We must quickly restore peace to the heart of old Lucas, something relatively easy in my view, for Juan López and Toñuelo are bursting to vouch for Señora Frasquita…'

'I don't need any man to vouch for me!' the latter replied. 'I have two much more credit-worthy witnesses who nobody can claim I have seduced or bribed…'

'And where are they?' asked the miller.

'They are downstairs, by the door…'

'Then tell them to come up; they have my permission.'

'The poor dears can't …'

'Ah, so they are two women… A trustworthy testimony!'

'No, they're not two women either. They are two females…'

'It gets worse! Must be two young girls!… Please tell me their names.'

'One's Pine Nut and the other's Light Touch…'

'Our two donkeys! Frasquita, you're making fun of me?'

'No, I'm quite serious. I can prove to you from the testimonies of our donkeys that I wasn't in the mill when you saw the magistrate there.'

'For God's sake explain yourself!…'

'And, Lucas… die of shame for ever doubting my honour! While you went from the village to our house tonight, I headed from our house to the village, and so our paths crossed. But you weren't on the path or, rather, had stopped to kindle sparks in the middle of a field…'

'True enough I stopped!… Go on.'

'At this your jenny hee-hawed…'

'Just so! Oh, I'm so happy!… Go on, go on, for your every word restores one year to my life!'

'Another hee-haw from the path answered that one…'

'Oh! Yes… yes!… Bless you! I can hear it now!'

'It was Light Touch and Pine Nut, who'd recognised each other and greeted one another like good friends, while we two didn't recognise or greet each other…'

'Not a word more! Not a word more!…'

'We didn't recognise each other to such an extent,' Señora Frasquita continued, 'that we both took fright and fled in opposite directions… So now you see I wasn't in the mill! If you want to know why you found the magistrate in our bed, feel these clothes you are wearing, and which must still be wet, and they'll tell you better than I can. His Honour fell into the mill race, and Ferret stripped him and put him in our bed! If you want to know why I opened the door… it was because I thought you were drowning and shouting to me. Finally, if you want to know about the appointment… But that's all I have to say for the moment. When we're by ourselves, I'll tell you about that and other things… that I don't like to mention in front of this lady.'

'Everything Señora Frasquita said is the pure truth!' shouted Juan López, wishing to ingratiate himself with Doña Mercedes, since she ruled over the magistrate's house.

'Every bit! Every bit!' added Toñuelo, toeing his master's line.

'Everything… so far!' added the magistrate, very pleased the Navarrese explanations hadn't gone any further.

'So you are innocent!' old Lucas exclaimed in the meantime, embracing the evidence. 'Frasquita! Dearest, dearest Frasquita! Forgive the injustice I've done you and let me hug you!…'

'That's another kettle of fish!…' retorted the miller's wife, withdrawing her body. 'Before I hug you, you must explain yourself…'

'I will explain for him and myself…' said Doña Mercedes.

'I've been waiting over an hour for you to do just that!' exploded the magistrate as he struggled to get to his feet.

'But I won't do any such thing,' his wife continued turning a contemptuous back on her husband, 'until these two gentlemen have changed their clothes… and even then, I'll only explain to those who deserve to hear explanations.'

'Let's go and change…' said the Murcian to the man from Madrid, very content he hadn't murdered him, but still regarding him with true Moorish hatred. 'Your Honour's clothes are suffocating me! I've felt wretched in them!…'

'Because you don't understand them!' replied the magistrate. 'On the contrary, I can't wait to get them back on, in order to hang you and half the world if I'm not satisfied by my wife's explanations!'

The magistrate's wife, on hearing these words, soothed the gathering with a gentle smile, proper to those hard-worked angels whose vocation it is to protect humanity.

34

The magistrate's wife is also beautiful

As soon as the magistrate and old Lucas left the room, his wife sat down on the sofa again, sat Señora Frasquita by her side, and, addressing the servants and officials gathered in the doorway, issued them with pleasantly simple orders:

'Come on, lads and lasses!… Tell this excellent woman all the bad things you know about me.'

The fourth estate stepped forward, and ten voices tried to speak at the same time; but the wet nurse, as the person with the most nous in the house, imposed silence on the others, and said what follows:

'You should know, Señora Frasquita, that My Ladyship and I were looking after the children tonight, waiting to see whether our master would come, and praying the third rosary to pass the time (for the reason Ferret gave was that the magistrate was in hot pursuit of some horrific brigands, and it wasn't right for us to go to bed before we'd seen him return home unharmed), when we heard the sound of people in the bedroom next door, which is where my master and mistress have their marriage bed. Frightened to death, we took the light and went to find out who was in the bedroom, when, ay, Virgen del Carmen!, we walked in and saw a man, dressed like my master, but who wasn't him (but was rather your husband!) trying to hide under the bed. "Thieves!" we started to scream, and a moment later the room was full of people, and the constables were dragging the would-be magistrate from his hiding place. My lady, who, like everyone else, recognised old Lucas, and saw him in that garb, feared he'd killed our master and began to lament in a way that would crack boulders... Meanwhile, the rest of us shouted, "Lock him up! Lock him up!" "Thief! Murderer!" were the nicest words old Lucas heard; and he stood by the wall, like a dead man, saying not a single word. But as they were taking him to prison, he said... something I'll repeat, although it would really be better to keep this quiet: "Madam, I am neither thief nor murderer: the thief and murderer... of my honour is in my house, and in bed with my wife."'

'Poor Lucas!' sighed Señora Frasquita.

'Woe is me!' murmured the magistrate.

'That's what we all said: "Poor old Lucas and poor Her Ladyship!" Because... the truth is, Señora Frasquita, we already had an inkling that our master had set his sights on you... though nobody imagined you...'

'Nurse!' exclaimed the magistrate's wife severely. 'Don't continue along that path!...'

'I will walk you along another...' intervened a constable, taking advantage of that break to resume the thread. 'Old Lucas (who cleverly tricked us with his clothes and the way he walked when he entered the house; so much so that we all took him to be the magistrate) hadn't come with the best of intentions, and if our Ladyship hadn't been up... imagine what might have happened...'

'What! You can shut up too!' the cook interrupted. 'You're just spouting nonsense! Yes, it's true, Señora Frasquita: old

Lucas was forced to confess the intentions he'd brought with him, to explain his presence in our mistress' bedroom… Our Ladyship couldn't restrain her anger when she heard him, and slapped him so hard on the mouth that half of what he wanted to say stuck there! Even I launched into a round of insults, and tried to take his eyes out… Because you know, Señora Frasquita, that, though he's your husband, the idea of coming with clean hands…'

'You're a good-for-nothing gossip!' shouted the porter, standing in front of that tribune. 'What else could you have expected?… In a word, Señora Frasquita, listen to me and let's get to the real truth. Her Ladyship did and said what she had to… but then, when her anger subsided, she took pity on old Lucas and noted the magistrate's bad behaviour and said these words or similar: "Whatever thoughts you harboured, old Lucas, and although I'll never be able to forgive such rudeness, your wife and my husband must be made to believe for a few hours they've been hoist by their own petard, and that you, helped by this disguise, have returned insult for injury. This deceit is the best form of revenge and we can easily stop when it suits us!" After they'd agreed this amusing stratagem, our Ladyship and old Lucas told us all that we had to do and say when His Honour returned; and I certainly gave Sebastian Ferret's backside a hiding I don't think he'll forget for a long time this night of St Simon and St Judas…'

By the time the porter stopped talking, the magistrate's wife and the miller's wife had been whispering for some time, kissing and hugging each other every minute, on occasion unable to stifle their laughter.

A pity we couldn't hear what they were saying!… But the reader can imagine what it was without too much effort, and if not the reader, at least the readeress.

An imperial decree

At this the magistrate and old Lucas returned to the room, each in his own clothes.

'Now it's my turn!' declared the illustrious Don Eugenio de Zuñiga.

After hitting his staff on the floor a couple of times as if to gather up energy (like the official Antaeus, who didn't feel strong until his rod of the Indies touched the ground)[11], he declared thunderously to his wife who was as cool as a cucumber:

'Merceditas… I am waiting for you to explain yourself!…'

Meanwhile, the miller's wife had got up and was giving old Lucas a pinch of peace that made him see stars, while she looked at him with bewitching, tranquil eyes.

The magistrate, observing the pantomime, was rooted to the spot, unable to explain such an *unmotivated* recon-ciliation.

He then addressed his wife a second time, spoke to her as sour as vinegar:

'Señora! Everyone's seeing eye to eye except for us! Assuage my doubts!… I order you to as your husband and as the magistrate!'

And he crashed his staff against the floor once more.

'Are you leaving?…' Doña Mercedes exclaimed, walking over to Señora Frasquita and ignoring Don Eugenio. 'Well, go without a care in the world, for this scandal will have no other consequence. Rosa! Light up this gentle couple's way, for they say they are about to leave… God go with you, old Lucas.'

'No!… No!…' shouted de Zuñiga, blocking their way. 'Old

Lucas is not going anywhere! He's under arrest till I get the whole truth! Hey, constables! In the King's name!…'

Not a single flunkey obeyed Don Eugenio. They all looked at his wife.

'Come on, my good man! Let the people through!' the latter added, almost treading on her husband, while bidding farewell to everyone most gracefully; that is, her head to one side, taking up her skirt with her fingertips and bowing elegantly, till she completed the extravagant curtsey which was all the rage at the time.

'But I… But you… But we… But they!…' the old man kept muttering, tugging at his wife's dress and upsetting her well-initiated curtsies.

In vain! Nobody took any notice of the magistrate!

As soon as everybody had gone, and the hapless spouses were left alone in the room, Doña Mercedes finally deigned to speak to her husband, in an accent which a tsarina of Greater Russia would have used to fulminate against a minister condemned to perpetual Siberian exile:

'If you live a thousand years, you'll never know what happened this night in my chamber… If you'd been there, as is proper, you wouldn't need to ask anyone. As far as I'm concerned, there is not, and will never be, any reason to oblige me to give you satisfaction, for I hold you in such contempt that if you weren't the father of my children, I'd throw you over this balcony right now, just as I'm now throwing you out of my bedroom for ever. So goodnight, my good man.'

After she'd said these words, which Don Eugenio heard without protest (for alone with his wife he didn't dare to), his wife went into the study, through the study to her bedroom, shut the doors behind her, and the poor man stood there jilted in his own front room, mumbling between his gums (not between his teeth) with unparalleled cynicism:

'Well, sir, I didn't expect to escape so lightly!… Ferret will find me a bed.'

3 6

Conclusion, moral and epilogue

The sparrows chirped their welcome to the dawn as old Lucas and Señora Frasquita left the city on their way to the mill.

The couple walked, and the two donkeys went before them tied together.

'On Sunday you must go to confession (the miller's wife was telling her husband), for you must cleanse yourself of all tonight's bad thoughts and criminal intentions…'

'You're quite right…' the miller answered. 'But, in the meantime, you must do me another favour, and give the mattress and sheets on our bed to the poor, and make it up anew. I'm not sleeping where that poisonous reptile sweated!'

'Don't even mention his name, Lucas!' retorted Señora Frasquita. 'Let's talk about something else. I hope I might deserve a second favour…'

'Your lips have only to ask…'

'This summer you must take me to the baths in Solán de Cabras.'

'Why?'

'To see if we can have children.'

'A magnificent idea! I'll take you, God willing.'

With this they reached the mill, just as the sun, which wasn't out yet, was gilding the peaks of the mountains.

In the afternoon, much to the surprise of the spouses, who

weren't expecting new visits from distinguished personages after the previous evening's scandals, more of the powers-that-be turned up than ever. The venerable prelate, a multitude of canons, the lawyer, two friars and other persons (it was later discovered they had been summoned there by His Most Illustrious Worship) filled the little square beneath the vine.

Only the magistrate was missing.

Once the gathering was complete, the bishop spoke first: that, though certain things had happened in that house, he and his canons would continue to visit it as before, so that neither the honourable miller, his wife, nor the other people present would share a public censure that was only deserved by the man whose torpid behaviour had profaned such a respectable, law-abiding assembly. He paternally exhorted Señora Frasquita in the future not to be so provocative and tempting in what she said or did and to try to cover more of her arms and wear her dress higher over her bosom; he advised old Lucas to be more disinterested, more circumspect and less immodest in the way he interacted with his superiors; and finally he bestowed his blessing on everyone and said that as he wasn't fasting that day, he really wanted to eat a couple of bunches of grapes.

They were all of the same opinion… in this respect… and the vine shook that afternoon. The miller reckoned it cost him two stones of grapes!

These hearty get-togethers went on for almost three years, until, against everybody's predictions, the armies of Napoleon entered Spain and the War of Independence was unleashed.

The bishop, the magistrate, and the director of penances died in 1808, and the lawyer and other devotees in 1809, 10, 11 and 12, as they couldn't stand the sight of those Frenchmen, Poles and other characters who invaded their land and smoked pipes in the church presbyteries during Mass for the troops!

The magistrate, who never returned to the mill, was deposed by a French *maréchal* and died in the main prison in Granada, because he refused for one moment (may it be said in His Honour) to compromise with the foreign power.

Doña Mercedes didn't remarry, and gave her children a perfect upbringing before retiring in old age to a convent, where she finished her days with a saintly reputation.

Ferret Frenchified.

Señor Juan López became a guerrilla fighter, then leader, and died, like the constable, in the famous Battle of Baza, after killing lots of Frenchmen.

Finally, old Lucas and Señora Frasquita (though they never managed to have children, despite going to Solán de Cabras and making many vows and pledges) continued to love each other in the same way, reached a very advanced age, and saw off Absolutism in 1812 and 1820, saw it re-appear in 1814 and 1832, until, finally the constitutional system was properly established after the death of the absolute monarch, and they went on to a better life (the instant the first Carlist war broke out), though the top hats people then wore could never make them forget *those years* symbolised by the three-cornered variety.

NOTES

1. Here, Alarcón refers respectively to St Anne, the mother of the Virgin Mary; Joseph, husband of the Virgin Mary; and Judith, whose story is told in the apocryphal Book of Judith. The widowed Judith defended her country by captivating the enemy, Holofernes, with her beauty, and taking advantage of the general's intoxication to cut off his head.

2. According to Greek mythology, Niobe boasted that she was better than Leto for having borne seven sons and seven daughters. They were eventually killed by Apollo and Artemis, the children of Leto, and Niobe herself was turned into stone.

3. Spanish painter of the Romantic period Francisco de Goya (1746–1828) became well known for his portraits of the Spanish aristocracy.

4. María Luisa of Parma (1751–1819) was the Queen Consort of Charles IV of Spain (1748–1819), and one of Goya's biggest patrons (see note 3). She also appeared as the subject of many of his paintings.

5. Francisco Gómez de Quevedo y Villegas (1580–1645) was a prolific Spanish writer, best known for his picaresque novel, *The Life of a Scoundrel* (trans, 1626).

6. Pomona was the Roman goddess of fruit and fruit trees.

7. 'An apology offered when not sought is an admission of guilt' (Latin).

8. 'Enough said, let there be no more speeches' (Latin).

9. '*De profundis*' are the first words of Psalm 130. Literally, they mean 'out of the depths' (Latin).

10. According to German legend, Mephistopheles was the name of the evil spirit to whom Faust sold his soul.

11. In the Greek myth, Antaeus, the son of Poseidon, was a champion wrestler. Each time he was thrown to the ground he arose stronger and more powerful than before, gaining his strength from contact with the earth.

Pedro Antonio de Alarcón was born in Guadix in Spain on 10th March 1833. After a brief education at a seminary, the young Alarcón began to read widely, teaching himself French and Italian. While still in Guadix, he established a journal dedicated to literature, the arts and the sciences. It was here that he published his early attempts at poetry. In 1853, just before his twentieth birthday, he moved to Madrid with the intention of becoming an established poet. However, he found little success, and after narrowly avoiding being drafted into the army, he moved again, this time to Granada, where he became involved in revolutionary politics. Back in Madrid, he was to become the editor of *El Látigo*, a fiercely Republican newspaper. In 1855, Alarcón appeared to renounce political journalism and left Spain for Paris. It was in the same year that he published his first novel, *El final de Norma*.

In 1859, Alarcón enrolled in the army as a volunteer and went to fight in the colonial campaign in Morocco. His account of his experiences, *Diario de un testigo de la guerra de Africa* [*Diary of a Witness to the War in Africa*] (1860), was a huge success, and is still regarded today as one of his most interesting works. After this triumph, he published an account of a trip through France, Switzerland and Italy. In 1866, he began to produce volumes of short stories, and in 1874, published perhaps his best-known book, *El sombrero de tres picos* [*The Three-Cornered Hat*]. This was followed by two further novels, *El escandalo* and *El nino de la Bola* in 1875 and 1880. *El Capitáin Veneno* [*Captain Venom*] appeared in 1881 and his last novel, *La prodiga*, the following year. Alarcon died on 19th July 1891, having suffered from partial paralysis for some time.

Peter Bush read Spanish literature at Cambridge and Oxford, before teaching Spanish in London comprehensive schools. He was subsequently Professor of Literary Translation at the Universities of Middlesex and East Anglia, where he directed the British Centre for Literary Translation for five years. His translations include fiction by Nura Amat, Juan Goytisolo and Juan Carlos Onetti; poetry by Jorge Yglesias and Orlando González Esteva, and screenplays by Pedro Almodóvar and Senel Paz. He has won the Valle-Inclán Prize for Literary Translation and an American Literary Translators Association Best Translation of the Year Award. He is the author of *Voice of the Turtle*, an anthology of Cuban stories, and vice-president of the International Translators Federation.

SELECTED TITLES FROM HESPERUS PRESS

Author	Title	Foreword writer
Louisa May Alcott	*Behind a Mask*	Doris Lessing
Jane Austen	*Love and Friendship*	Fay Weldon
Honoré de Balzac	*Colonel Chabert*	A.N. Wilson
Charles Baudelaire	*On Wine and Hashish*	Margaret Drabble
Aphra Behn	*The Lover's Watch*	
Charlotte Brontë	*The Green Dwarf*	Libby Purves
Mikhail Bulgakov	*The Fatal Eggs*	Doris Lessing
Miguel de Cervantes	*The Dialogue of the Dogs*	Ben Okri
Anton Chekhov	*Three Years*	William Fiennes
Wilkie Collins	*Who Killed Zebedee?*	Martin Jarvis
Arthur Conan Doyle	*The Tragedy of the Korosko*	Tony Robinson
William Congreve	*Incognita*	Peter Ackroyd
Joseph Conrad	*Heart of Darkness*	A.N. Wilson
Joseph Conrad	*The Return*	Colm Tóibín
Daniel Defoe	*The King of Pirates*	Peter Ackroyd
Marquis de Sade	*Incest*	Janet Street-Porter
Charles Dickens	*The Haunted House*	Peter Ackroyd
Charles Dickens	*A House to Let*	
Fyodor Dostoevsky	*The Double*	Jeremy Dyson
Fyodor Dostoevsky	*Poor People*	Charlotte Hobson
George Eliot	*Amos Barton*	Matthew Sweet
Henry Fielding	*Jonathan Wild the Great*	Peter Ackroyd
F. Scott Fitzgerald	*The Rich Boy*	John Updike
Gustave Flaubert	*Memoirs of a Madman*	Germaine Greer
E.M. Forster	*Arctic Summer*	Anita Desai
Elizabeth Gaskell	*Lois the Witch*	Jenny Uglow
Nikolai Gogol	*The Squabble*	Patrick McCabe
Thomas Hardy	*Fellow-Townsmen*	Emma Tennant
L.P. Hartley	*Simonetta Perkins*	Margaret Drabble

Charterhouse Library

56983